WORLD BUILDER

LUCAS KITCHEN

**LUCAS
KITCHEN
BOOKS**

LUCASKITCHEN.COM

ALSO BY LUCAS KITCHEN

Fiction

For The Sake Of The King | Isolation | Missionary To Mars | Cloud Haven | Divine Children | World Builder | Infinite Tomorrow

Children's Fiction

Good Enough | Adventures Beyond Mudville | Below The Huber Ice | Evan Wants To Go To Heaven

Non-Fiction

Salvation And Discipleship | Eternal Life | Eternal Rewards | Naked Grace | In Pursuit Of Fruit | Eternal Clarity | Things Above | Thomas Hero Of The Faith

All Available At: Lucaskitchen.com

MISSION

RUTH'S BLUE IRISES WERE islands surrounded by milky white. Her body was tight with tension. She continued to stare down at her work while a belligerent lock of hair hung unkempt across her features. Her soft, rounded face was attractive and kind, but her fashion sense had left a long time ago. It had never returned. The mismatched shades of her asymmetrical outfit complemented her colorful personality.

She stood, half bent over a desk littered with papers. A worldwide navigation chart dominated the tabletop clutter. She was no cartographer, but her mission required a unique map. It had a distinct look of something hand-printed. She had penned it all in a dark black ink that bit deep into the oversized page.

At various locations, red Xs stood lonesome. Like a pirate's map, the vibrant red marks hid an elusive mystery.

Unfortunately, she was either too dense or too tired to see it.

The Xs were spaced across the entire globe except for one isolated location. At this particular spot, there were so many marks that they had worn through the paper. This inky gash in the map gaped somewhere in the mid-north-east of North America.

The desk was not the only cluttered space in Ruth's workspace. Being an abandoned attic, its wood floor was rough and unfinished. There was a single shaft of light streaming in from a high, perched opening in the wall.

Her hand slammed against the firm surface of the desk. A few papers retreated from the rush of air. How could she have made such a reckless mistake?

Her hand trembled from the adrenaline her anger provided. In one fluid motion, she dropped to a sitting position in front of the desk. She used to love sitting on the floor. She could sit for hours. That is when Truss was present. She would sit quietly as Truss would teach her what he had learned on his latest adventure. The embers of passion in his eyes would spark a forest fire in her mind. His passion had enveloped her dark world. He had been the one who first taught her about the worlds beyond. He was the only one she had ever loved, and now she had lost him. She chuckled at the double meaning.

"I've lost my lover," She said with a silly smile. "And I can't remember where I've put him." Her short laugh turned into fat, salty tears.

She could not imagine what the council would do to her when they found out what she had done. From her sitting position, she flopped flat on her back. Her search was impossible. So she lay on the wooden planks. She was out of ideas. Despite the fact that her mind was empty, her task remained. She had to find Truss.

An explosion of light and sound rocked the old wooden boards she lay on. She shut her eyes, knowing what this must be. A time-space burst so intense could only be an interstellar jump. It meant they had come for her. They would find her guilty. Who knows what her punishment would be? The fear of her mistake lay on top of her so weighty she could not rise. She could not open her eyes. She could not even breathe.

Heavy footsteps knocked across the rickety old floor. Maybe there wouldn't be a trial. Maybe this is my executioner. She found this all the more reason to continue to lie motionless. Her eyes stayed sealed as the footsteps came unbearably close.

A dark, cello-like voice greeted her ears. At least he has a good voice, I'd hate for the last voice I hear to be scratchy and annoying, she thought. She passed another moment behind her eyelids before she realized he had spoken. She tried to recall what the voice had said. Something rigid poked at her shoulder from the direction where the footsteps had stopped.

"Are you well?" the voice came again. She warmed a bit to think of a kind executioner. She had to see this embodiment of irony.

She peeked through the smallest slit she could make in her eyelids. Recognition hit her as hard as if this visitor had dropped a brick on her head. It was Atromus, the Head of the Galactic Builders Council. The council was a federation covering thirty-six galaxies. It was strange that they had not sent a messenger. Why would they send the chairman of the GBC, she wondered. His face shifted gears from concern to confusion.

In one graceless movement, Ruth shot up from the floor. She straightened her mismatched clothes and fluffed her hair. She gave a slight bow of respect. She had never spoken to him. In fact, she had never even spoken to his assistant. She had thus far only ever talked to Atromus' assistant's assistant.

Atromus's appearance would be formidable in any world and in any majestic setting. By contrast, the place he stood at that moment only emphasized his immensity. A hint of smoke and heat rose from his shoulders and the top of his head. She knew this was the result of long-distance space-time bending. The dark black cloak that he wore acted as a shield for the tremendous heat created by such a use of power.

"May I take your coat?" She asked trying to be hospitable. It was impossible to remove the nervous note from her voice.

"No. It is quite all right. It will be over soon," He said as he spun around to look at the attic. Her mind raced at his words. It sounded ominous. She grasped for words, trying to keep the conversation going.

"How was your trip?" She asked. What a silly question. She was floundering.

He brushed his shoulders off with his hands and straightened his cloak. "The galactic weather is unpredictable this time of cycle. I had to jump through a Hydrogen Nebula. There was no way around it."

He kept his hair cropped short. His chiseled features now masked any emotion. His angular brow furrowed as if he was at least a little disappointed in the accommodations. She could scream.

"I do some of my best thinking while lying on the floor," She said with an awkward smile. Atromus gave her a raised eyebrow. She regretted the stupid comment. She stared at the floorboards, trying to think. Once again, her mind was empty. She wished Truss was there. He would know what to say. He always handled galactic dignitaries with such grace and poise.

What would Truss say, she thought. She lowered her voice a little and pretended to be him.

"I'm sorry, I didn't expect anyone to come, especially not..." she trailed off, trying to think of his formal title. Instead, shifted gears. She glanced at her wrist, where there was no watch. "I must have miscalculated, I didn't expect..." This time, it was he who cut her off.

He put his hand up to stop her. "Thank you for letting me shut up," she didn't say. He had the ease of a man used to obedience. His bright, powerful voice filled her with awe as he spoke.

"I'm here on somewhat of an unscheduled nature. How is the progress? I trust the research is coming along as planned?" He spun around the room once more. This time, he leaned over the desk to look at the papers that she had scattered there.

She rushed to organize the desk's contents. That is at least what she hoped he would perceive. In actual fact she made a point to cover up the map, knowing it would be uncomfortable to explain. She braced herself and tried to seem upbeat.

"The progress is—Well, it's—" She could not lie, but there were times when it would be so much easier. With reluctance, she continued. "We—I mean, I had a little set-back." She was ready to explain the entire situation when he interrupted her once more. This time, it was a welcome reprieve.

"I'm sure you will sort it out. Now on to the reason I've come." She could hardly hold back her relief. She knew she would have to answer for her mistake, but she would put it off as long as possible. He breathed deeply as if in preparation for a briefing. Again, he spoke with a rumbling tone. "We have a project for you two. We like your previous work. It's all creative, and most importantly, stable. This would be a great opportunity for you and your builder. It's an order of magnitude larger than anything you've done before, but we know that you both are ready."

She swallowed hard and breathed in her disbelief. To keep her composure, she needed to busy her hands. Write something her mind offered. She turned to her quill and inkwell on the desk. On a piece of scrap paper, she poised her fingers. Trying to sound casual, she managed to croak out, "How big?"

"It should be 900 trillion tons, give or take, radioactive molten core, and two orbiters. It's going to be in premium real estate. This project will also require a new star ignition. You two have done a star fire ignition, haven't you?" Atromus asked. Her thoughts piled up like train cars in a crash. Her heart began to race. Her palms grew sweaty. The ink pooled at the point where her quill stood motionlessly. She tried to say something.

"Uh. Well. No. We have never done a star fire ignition. My builder knows how, but—" Ruth choked.

"That's fine. It's all quite basic. Once you finish your assignment here, visit headquarters. You'll need a set of ignition schematics," He said.

"Yes, of course. Schematics."

He spoke again. "I know it's big, but we have admired your work for quite a while, and we know you're ready." He paused and stepped forward a pace. "There is one more thing, there will be inhabitants. Not just inhabitants but sentient ones. It's top secret, so this stays between us for now, but some will be..." He paused, searching for the right word. "immigrants and some indigenous born."

This was beyond words. In her wildest dreams, she never imagined that she could be on such an important build team. A few deep breaths gave her time to gather her frazzled wits. Finally composed enough to speak, she looked up.

"Wow, that will be a sight to see."

"Yes, it will be a great accomplishment; the history of an entire world rests on your work." Feelings of joy and pain washed over her as she remembered. They had lived through so many years of hoping for this moment. Now, her colossal mistake would ruin it all. He looked at his wrist, which did have a watch on it.

"Of course, this will all mean a bump in his schedule. We have to get ahead of this if we want to make it work."

"How much of a bump?" She tried to sound optimistic, but knew it did not matter what the schedule was. She was short one builder.

"Where are we?" He asked, not as if he didn't know, but because he wanted to be reminded.

She matched his tone, "Milky, Sol system, 3rd planet." He looked up at the unfinished ceiling, pondering her answer.

He asked, "One moon?" She nodded her head in compliance. "Ok let's say a month." Attempting to hide her concerns she smiled sheepishly and again nodded her head.

He turned and began straightening his cloak in preparation for his departure. As he made himself ready for his return journey, he questioned her idly. "Has he found a city yet?" Her mind raced, trying to think of a way to answer that would not reveal she had no idea where her builder was.

"You know how they jump around, it's hard to imagine where he might go next." She hoped that was good enough to suffice. He stopped smoothing his cloak for a moment as if something had just occurred to him. She felt as if she were on the edge of a cliff. He was about to ask her the question that would reveal the truth. His stoic look beamed through her. His response was emotionless.

"That's true until he finds a city. Your legwork will be much less once he gets acquainted with the sights and sounds. The smell is what drew me in. Every builder is different, but once he sets his sights on a city, it's where he will stay until his time is up." Her eyes widened. For the first time, it was not out of frustration but realization.

Watching for her reaction, Atromus displayed an empathetic smile. He stepped closer to her and put his hand on her shoulder. He spoke soft and bright. "It's a good idea to pull him from the field as soon as possible. Now that his official time is up, the bound ones of Molgathra can reach him. Keep him safe until you are able to restore him. We will see you soon. " He stepped back, prepped himself, and added, "For the sake of the King." An explosion of light, and he was gone.

She imagined the bound ones finding him. He was wide open now that he was no longer under celestial guard. She knew that she must, but it had never been so urgent that she find him. A sparkling hope twinkled in the back of her mind.

What had he said about the city? Why had she not thought of that? It was the most valuable information she had received in the hunt for her builder. She had been trying to anticipate Truss's moves. Her ground game was about to change. If Atromus was right, she finally had a new hope.

She returned to her desk and began gathering up her papers. She had work to do.

THE OBSERVER

THE IMAGE OF A busy ant hill reflected in a strange man's deep brown eyes. This was because the tip of his nose was hovering five centimeters from the upper peak of an active ant bed.

He had a proper top hat of the blackest velvet. A bow tie and a vest worked together in a fashionable ensemble. His outfit was high fashion of the late 1800's.

The delicious afternoon sun was shining on a small clearing. The man kneeled, leaning forward on his hands. He watched in breathless observation. The wild ant bed offered a stark contrast to the stillness in this peaceful forest.

The ants danced together as they rushed to finish the day's work. A smile began to tiptoe across the observer's face. After letting the expression saturate his eyes, he chuckled. He cooed a slight sound of discovery.

He had been trying to understand the weight-bearing limitations of the little creatures. He had only half considered the mystery for a few long moments when the answer came.

A mathematical equation unfolded across his mind. It explained the miniature creature's ability to do mighty works. He had no idea where these kinds of thoughts came from. Though, it was a thrill when a mystery unraveled itself with so little effort.

Now that he had discovered the secret of the ant's strength, it was time to record his findings. Moving to an upright position, he unfastened the top button on his dress coat. He pulled a small book and pencil from a hidden inner pocket.

The pencil had the distinct handmade markings of an artisan. The book was leather-bound and full of jagged-edged pages.

He began thumbing through the book in search of an open writing space. Page after page breezed by, revealing the diligent work of a tireless observer. He had packed every page with handwritten notes. Each drawing had perfectly dimensioned lines. The pencil depictions covered a range of animals and plants. He paused on a two-page spread with an illustration of a roaring bear. He smiled at the memory.

He continued to flip through the handwritten pages again. The observer's thumbs finally came to rest on the last page of the book. It was the only paper that remained blank.

With inhuman speed, his hand was set in motion. Within a few seconds, he filled the page with two drawings of ants. A sprawl of text accompanied every sketch. When he reached the last line of the hand-pulped paper, he stopped. He stood, dusted his knees off with his free hand, and fastened the top jacket button.

The jagged sound of a car horn gouged into the peaceful silence of his hidden glade. Now that his attention was free to wander, a flood of city sound rushed in. The city drenching every inch of the city park with a battery of noise pollution.

The sudden loss of silence did not affect the man. He looked out from the hill where he had been working. A massive metropolis begged for his observation. He was a man of undivided focus, but the city could evade his attention no longer. With so many things to name and catalog, he almost felt giddy; something he had not felt in over a century.

His free hand moved to the top of his hat. He applied ever so little pressure with an open palm, as a man would on a gusty day. He took a deep breath, closed his eyes, and vanished with a flash of light.

The ants still moved. The breeze still blew. The sun still shone. The city sounds still sang their sharp melodies. However, the observer was gone; no exit path, just gone.

CRAZY

A BALL POINT PEN tapped an agitated rhythm on a stack of papers laying in a tan file folder. The sleeve a white lab coat rimmed the hand. There was no reason Dr. Thomas needed to wear the traditional doctor's apparel. Yet, he appreciated the credibility that his attire offered.

His bleach white tennis shoes were always tied with exactly equal lengths of shoelace. His hair part was a thing of precise symmetry running like a fault line down his scalp. Like most doctors, he had no trouble inflating the value of his own time. He would make a patient wait for hours while he took an extended lunch. Despite all that, It annoyed Dr. Thomas to have to wait.

The room that the doctor was waiting in was bland. Its walls had the spectral variety of schoolhouse chalk. A folding table rested in the exact center of the room. It created an irritating tone as his pen bounced. On both sides of the table sat brown padded chairs, one of which Dr. Thomas was occupying.

He thought of all the patients he had seen across this table. His thoughts then wandered to dinner. His wife was making Stromboli, which meant he would not be working late tonight. He glanced left to the reflection in the window. It pleased him that his part had not moved since he had left his bathroom mirror.

The window was thick one-way glass. It allowed a team of anonymous specialists to peer in as a session was taking place. At least, that's what he wanted the patients to think. It was a guarded secret that there was no observation room on the other side. The promise of onlookers gave Dr. Thomas an advantage over his violent patients. This is why he had the window to nowhere installed. It also doubled as a mirror, which he used often.

The truth was much more dismal. Shady Oak Mental Hospital was too understaffed to provide any protective oversight. As soon as an orderly delivered one patient to his appointment, he would be off to see to some other matter. The lack of sufficient personnel was the reason today's patient was late. So Dr. Thomas continued to rap on the table with his writing pen.

The doctor wondered who he had next. His preparedness was almost unnecessary. He knew his guests as if they were old family friends, although he rarely treated them as such.

He shuffled some papers without interest and recognized his own handwriting. Name: James Hershowitz. Age: 28. Symptoms: schizophrenic episodes, delusions of grandeur, memory dysfunction. Dr. Thomas smiled.

Although he would never say it aloud, this patient was as crazy as a loon. He was completely delusional. He lacked any ability to discern reality from his own psychotic creations. Dr. Thomas absolutely loved meeting with James.

James had an uncanny ability to entertain. His visions were legendary among the staff. It was so rare to find someone whose delusions were so coherent, not to mention entertaining. The age of psychotropic drugs and specialized diagnosis' had changed things. Dr. Thomas missed the good ole' days when he could call his patients what they were, "crazy." Everything now was a depressive disorder, attachment-aversion or learned behavioral dysfunction.

This was untrue of James. He was deliciously insane, and Dr. Thomas loved it. He wished the board would allow him to do electro-shock treatment, Hydroblast therapy, or Lobotomy. Those were the main reasons psychiatry drew him in. What he wouldn't give to put James between the electrodes and zap him with 48 volts. He grinned at the image. He still kept a shock therapy kit in the basement. All the industry would allow was sit in front of this fake window, and remind him to take his prescriptions. He huffed at his bad luck. James would at least give him some stories to share with the boys at the tennis club.

A double wrap at the door signaled the beginning of his appointment. The well-worn knob creaked as it spun. The crack revealed a tentative eye gazing through. The arrival of the patient made Dr. Thomas long for his lobotomy scalpel.

James pushed the door open and waddled in. The orderly closed the door behind him. He was not obese, but Dr. Thomas had made fun of thinner men for their weight.

The blue cotton outfit squeezed James' midsection. Dr. Thomas thought he looked like a ham sandwich with too little bread. His plastic rimmed black glasses contained a set of thick lenses of different strengths. He had astigmatism in his right eye and near perfect vision in his left. The difference in corrective power made his eyes look as if they were different sizes.

James wore an inappropriate goofy smile for the occasion. This made Dr. Thomas bubble with anticipation. James' hair looked like an overused rug. The smile widened as he approached his assigned seat. The brown folding chair rasped across the bare floor as James poured himself into it.

"Hey, Doc. Have you been taking your medicine?" James said, giggling to himself. Dr. Thomas could see the tickle of delight as it worked through James like a shiver. He was going to enjoy this. It was rare for Dr. Thomas to share a laugh, but he reached into his rarely used comical repertoire and pulled out a gem.

"I know you haven't been taking your prescriptions, James?" Dr. Thomas said.

"How do you know?" James asked.

"Because I've been trying to poison you for months," Dr. Thomas laughed bounced with his joke. James stared back as Dr. Thomas laughed alone. He could see that he had made James uncomfortable with his hilarious joke. His tennis buddies would love that one. This time, he used his formal tone. When the doctor's chuckle piped down, he straightened the papers in front of him.

James fixed his stare to the ceiling. Dr. Thomas glanced up to see what he was looking at. A moth fluttered around the buzzing light bulb. Dr. Thomas snapped his fingers to get his patients attention. James returned his stare to the doctor. His eyes looked like the broken headlights of an abandoned car.

Looking at his notes once more, Dr. Thomas asked,"Have you been taking your meds?"

"No Doc! I've been taking your meds!" This time is was James' turn to laugh alone. Dr. Thomas was confident his own joke had been ten times as funny. His pudgy patient removed his glasses and wiped them with the corner of his hospital shirt. Dr. Thomas prepared to move forward.

"I really don't need them anymore. I am as clear as I've ever been." Dr. Thomas' annoyance died as he watched James posture himself. Taking some papers in his hand and glancing down at them for the effect he spoke with too much articulation.

"I'm glad to hear that Mr. Hershowitz." As if he was learning something from the pages, he scanned them another moment. "Why don't you tell me a little bit more about your story?"

Now it was James' smile that faded. The doctor loved making his patients uncomfortable. This was especially true with the ones who were most likely to snap. James fidgeted in his chair for a long moment. He looked around the room until his eyes caught sight of the moth once more. The doctor snapped his fingers and said, "Why don't you start by telling me how old you are?"

"I guess..." James trailed off deep in thought. He started again. "I guess in Earth years I'd be around one thousand nine hundred and seventy-five. Of course, I wasn't on this planet for most of that time. I've only been in this solar system a few hundred."

James watched the moth with his eyes but kept his head forward. Dr. Thomas gave him his trademark lifeless stare. Silently Dr. Thomas was begging for more. Give me the good stuff, He thought as he waited. He hoped for a whopper to share with his tennis buddies.

"And how exactly did you get to this planet?" Dr. Thomas' professional demeanor was a thing of legend. A lack of emotion would give James a desire verify his delusions. It was a trick the doctor used often. He was brimming with anticipation at James' next tasty tidbit of fabrication. James glanced at the window in the wall.

"Can you tell them to turn off the camera? This is kind of a secret." Dr. Thomas spun around and gave the window a gesture. He smiled as he drug his flat hand across his throat. This signaled his imaginary assistant to turn off the imaginary camera. The doctor turned back around and gave James his undivided attention. He was giddy with expectation although his calm exterior betrayed no hint.

"I will show you." James stood from his chair and looked down at the doctor with an excited stare. Here it comes, the doctor thought. "I like to take a deep breath before I do it," he said with a grin.

In a familiar fashion, James placed his hand on the top of his head, took a deep breath, closed his eyes and stood still. A leathery grin stretched across Dr. Thomas' face when nothing happened.

"Brilliant," Dr. Thomas said. "You're quite good at standing still with your hand on your head."

James opened a tentative eye. He closed his eye, took a deep breath and tried again. Dr. Thomas spoke with a calculated measure of incredulity.

"Thank you, James, you've shown me all I need to see for today."

THE CITY

THE BUSTLING NOISE AND quick movement echoed off the hard surfaces. The city sound made for a rhythm that was unique. Layered civilization had a particular kind of pattern.

The observer had stayed away from cities since his earliest memories. The wild places of Earth had attracted him. He found nature peaceful and serene. There was something magical about observing and cataloging trees and ants. The concrete jungle that he now stood in was overwhelming. He didn't know where to start.

"They need a name," He said to himself. It wasn't like anyone could hear him. He thumbed through his new sketchbook. He had already filled a few pages, and it was only mid-morning. He pushed his pencil across the page. He considered what he would call this unique group of creatures.

"Large brain builders," He tried. It wasn't artistic, but it did describe them well enough. He wasn't ready to commit, but he needed a working title. As he spelled out the name across the top of the page, he said, "I might change it once I get to know you better."

For most of the afternoon, he moved through the streets and alleyways. When someone intrigued him, which was about every five seconds, he would get close. He stood nose to nose with the large brain builders, trying to glean whatever he could. Being invisible had its advantages. Their eyes stared through at every pass. With each glance, gait, and gesture, there was more to write and sketch. He could hardly keep up with the river of data.

Down the street, he saw shops filled to the ceiling with merchandise on full shelves. He bobbed into a busy store with huge glass windows. He watched the salesman and customers doing their materialistic dance. He sketched what he could of the rapid interactions. After a few moments of observation, he thought he understood their activities. He wrote in his book.

"The large brain builders (I shall notate them as LBB henceforth). The LBBs like to carry various items. It seems to be part of an elaborate mating ceremony. When one of the LBBs finds an item they wish to carry, they bring it to the front of the shop. Each has a miniature rectangular

platter with letters and numbers on it. They pass the rectangular platter near a machine. I speculate that the machine calculates the LBB's carrying capacity. If all is clear, the attendant then places the item in an unneeded bag. The attendant then hangs the bag on one of the LBB's available appendages. The LBB then leaves the shop. P.S. The bag is what confuses me the most. The LBB can carry the item to the front of the shop easily enough. Why they then need a carrying case baffles me. There is certainly much more to learn."

He finished his entry with a sketch of a woman sliding her credit card in one hand, and a shopping sack in the other. He shadowed that shopper for most of an hour. With each store she went into, he became more confused. He tried to make sense of it with another entry in his sketchbook.

"The female LBB has entered and exited no less than 12 unique shops. Each time, she failed to exit with less than she had entered the shop. Hypothesis: Soon, the machine will inform her she has reached her carrying capacity, due to the numerous bags that she carries. They are now the only way of cataloguing where each item came from. There are too many mysteries to unravel all at once."

He created another sketch next to where he had jotted down his findings. Before he could congratulate himself for solving the mystery, he second-guessed his hypothesis. These large brain builders were more complicated than he had expected. He would have followed the shopper into another store, but something grabbed his attention.

Down the sidewalk, about ten paces away, was something small, alive, and moving slowly. He felt the rise of blood pressure and the growing infatuation. As his eyes widened, he moved with a predator's speed to get a better look. He dropped to his knees. He hovered over a snail moving painfully slow across the hot sidewalk. He had seen many of these creatures before. He had not expected to find one so far from the wild places of the planet.

His mind raced. How could this gastropod live here? The excitement of finding the unexpected gave him great joy. He watched the little creature as his infatuation rose to a fever pitch. He pulled out his notebook and sketched the snail. Next to it, he wrote another entry.

"Glory of glories! I admire the the LBB's ability to live in harmony with the lower creatures. It fills me with wonder to imagine how they have communicated with this species. They must have some ground traffic control system. Coordinating the safety of such small life with that of the LBBs is a tremendous achievement. I feel my respect for the LBBs growing."

The observer had been so enthralled with the snail that he had blocked out all activity around him. That is until a size ten and a half, dirty, tennis shoe slapped down on the pavement. This would not have been of any interest except that the snail was between the shoe and the concrete.

Being so close to this sudden slaughter knocked the observer back on his hands. He could not believe what he had just seen. He thought it must have been a mistake. He looked up at the body attached to the shoe. He knew at once it was no mistake. This male of the large brain builder clan did not intend to eat this lower creature. In fact, it was evident that he was not even aware of the needless destruction of life.

The observer scratched a thick, dark line through "large brain builders." He jotted his correction below the marked-out name. He wrote, "careless bringers of death." The observer had a new subject of observation. He stood and began to follow the snail killer.

CREEPER

THE SNAIL KILLER HAD the look of a street creep. Above the battered shoes, a pair of tattered jeans covered his legs. He wore a red cotton t-shirt with some unimportant symbol on it. His pace showed him to be unaware of the accepted sidewalk etiquette.

Within minutes, the observer had completely pushed the death of the snail out of his mind. He had found a new infatuation, and how infatuated he was. With every step, a river of data was pouring out of this strange human creature. He kept his book in hand and wrote furiously as the man plodded the pavement.

"The Street Creep Slows his pace. He's caught sight of a female of the same species. The creep watches with deep intensity. He matched his pace to the woman."

The Observer turned his attention to the female. He was trying to understand what caught the attention of the street creep. He continued to write at a maddening speed.

"The LBB female is displaying some strange characteristics. She has squeezed her voluminous figure into a clothing size that would be more appropriate for younglings. Her footwear is oddly shaped as well. Her elevated heel rides atop a spike protruding from the bottom of her shoe. This gives an unpredictable warble to her walk. I speculate that her apparel choice is intended to ward off possible mates. No potential mate would procreate with a female unable to choose proper clothing sizes. Her tight clothing should be enough to scare away the street creep. It will be interesting to see what happens."

He watched for another few seconds when an idea occurred to him. He began to write once more.

"Is it possible that this is not a mating ceremony at all? I speculate that the street creeper is stalking his prey. He has seen the female's unbalanced warbling. Has he identified her as his next meal? I'm bubbling with excitement."

A strange, high-pitched sound mixed with the city noise. It was somewhat like a bird song but more brittle. The woman, now standing still in the midst of a moving hustle, noticed the sound as well.

With the sound still ringing out, she reached into her bag and produced from it a small metallic object. Her free hand hung from her wrist like a loose branch after a storm. He noticed the resemblance between her fingernails and a bird's beak. They were long and sharp. She then put the device to her ear.

The woman began to speak. Baffled, the observer removed his top hat and scratched his head with the tip of his pencil. Her squelchy voice crackled from the loud hole in her face with a bitter timbre. The pitch was much too high for a mammal of her size.

"I told you, Gary, I don't want a red Corvette. You know I can't stand American-made. Corvettes are for bald losers like you. If you don't love me enough to get a…"

Listening to her conversation was like standing beneath a bird as it poops. His respect for the large-brained builders was quickly eroding. She contorted her face in ways he had not yet seen. She began scratching out another rancid smattering of speech.

"Whatever! If you just made more money, we wouldn't have to make these kinds of decisions!"

With tremendous speed, a red blur burst into the observer's vision. He had almost forgotten the street creeper. The mystery of why he was stalking the female was both remembered and solved in an instant.

In one swift and experienced motion, the creep grabbed the woman's handbag. He removed it from her shoulder with force as he bolted. It was like puzzle pieces falling into place. The observer wrote in his book once more.

"I have solved the mystery! As I have said before, the LBBs like carrying things. The street creeper saw that the female had more to carry than he did. He acquired the female's bag so that he might carry it himself. She will be pleased to allow the creeper to carry her bag since her tight clothes and unbalanced shoes restrict her motion."

The observer glanced up to test his hypothesis. He realized at once that he was wrong once again. The female began screaming for help. With every step the creep put between them, she increased her volume.

A rush of emotion poured over him. It was as if for a brief moment, he was not simply an observer. He watched as the female belted a squawking plea. He saw her tears. He sensed her fear. As unaccustomed to this activity as he was, he realized he felt for her. Empathy drenched him as he watched the scene unfold. He had to understand. He had to know how he could feel so connected to a creature that was so unfamiliar.

In the fervor of the moment, he acted almost without thought. He tucked his pencil behind his ear, lifted his hand high in the air, and snapped his fingers. Everything around him paused. He had done this before in the midst of nature, but never had it been so dramatic. The city scene, with all its noise and circumstance, came to a halt.

A dynamic silence replaced the battery of city sounds. All stood still.

Finally, some peace. Now he could think. He could unravel the mystery. His footsteps marked the silent scene as he walked toward the female. She was statue-like, frozen in time. He planted his feet toe to toe with her. He placed his nose centimeters away from hers and began his research.

What is this creature? Being so close, he could almost feel the emotion painting her face. Her cheeks were still wet with her own salty tears. The communication device was still in her hand. She was stone still as if forced to relive the same moment over and over.

After a moment of contemplation, he pulled the pencil from behind his ear. He opened his book and began to pen her pain. He had been looking at it all wrong. He had assumed that these creatures were like the beasts he had encountered in the wild. He had considered them as intelligent animals. He saw now that they were deeper than that. They were crafted after a complex image. What a mystery they were.

A second later, he had her face, another second still, a paragraph on her facial expressions. Below the sketch, he penciled the words,

"Violated. Helpless. Abandoned. Wants to love and be loved."

His pencil trailed at the end of the phrase. How could he see it so clearly? There was something missing. These creatures had a profound longing unlike any of the wild animals he had seen. Where does this longing come from? How have they become so bent? In all the years he had spent on the planet, he had thought he was studying the most exotic creatures. However, he had ignored the only race that spoke a language he knew. It was a language that lay long dormant in his soul. It was the language of emotion. Still, he was unsure what to do with this frozen scene.

He spent another two minutes in close proximity with the female before he moved on to the street creeper. His timid approach was like one entering a sleeping child's room. He did not want to upset the delicate balance of emotion at play. Once again with pencil and book at the ready, he squared off with the motionless creeper also frozen in time.

His frozen stride displayed an athletic ability born more out of fear than recreation. The creeper had narrowly missed a street sign by half a meter.

The creeper's face was stolid, but he thought he sensed more beneath the rigid facade. The man's eyes were like mysterious pools now carved in timeless stone. With incredible speed, the observer cast a pencil image of the man. Underneath the picture, he wrote,

"Rejected. Afraid. Hungry."

The scene began to unravel and organize itself in his mind. These were not enemies. They are creatures in need of resources. Their need for resources was in conflict with their need for acceptance and love. In a moment, his emotion was gone. He thought about how fickle the substance of emotion was.

He was cautious not to disturb the location of the handbag hanging from the creeper's hand. He could see that there were a few personal items. Reaching into the purse, he pulled out its contents.

He recognized the credit card at once. Along with it, a handful of cash. He had seen people throughout the day trade cash for items to carry. He returned all the female's belongings to the bag except for the cash. He sensed from the victim's emotional outburst that the items in the bag were of personal value to her.

A slight smile broke across his face. Careful not to touch the Creep's hand, he slid the money into the man's clenched fist. He stepped back to look at the creep now with the cash tucked tightly in his grip.

He then took the strap of the handbag and unclasped it on one side. The strap that he now held was a soft, rich leather, not unlike the cover of the books that he carried. The observer then wrapped the handbag strap around the nearby signpost. He reconnected the other end of the strap to the purse. Although the bag was in the creep's hand, it was now also connected to a one-way street sign. He glanced at the female and back at the creeper.

He raised his hand high in the air and once again snapped his fingers. The scene exploded back to action. It felt like a concussion of sound and life. It all happened at once. The creep, still in motion, realized that the stolen bag in his hand was connected to a street sign. Another step, and he was at his full arm's reach. The tension wrenched his arm hard. In the same moment, his own momentum jerked the bag from his hand. The bag hit the pavement but was still strapped to the signpost.

A second of indecision crossed his features as he paused. He was trying to decide which path to follow: grab the bag, or make a run for it. In a quick motion, he reached out his arm to go for the bag, only to realize that there was already something in his hand. With surprise, he opened his fist to find a wad of cash. His eyes widened, his feet once again changed course, and he ran.

Within seconds, the female was there, still blathering into her communication device. She reached down for her bag as he heard her speaking.

"I don't know, one second he was running with it, and the next it was wrapped around a street sign."

The flood of realization washed over him. He had just done something new. He never had, in all his remembered years, interfered with a subject. He could not decide if he should be proud or appalled. Could he even still consider himself an observer? He placed his hand on his hat, closed his eyes, took a deep breath and vanished.

THE CHAIN

Ruth didn't know where Truss was, but she had a good idea where to look. The red ink had been pointing her toward him for the last few weeks. She had her maps rolled neatly and stowed in her backpack. If the head of the Galactic Builder's Council was right, then Truss would be in a City. It hadn't taken long to overlay a map of human cities over her own chart. She could have bitten her own ear. It was so obvious.

She stood motionless in the middle of the street. It was the largest city she'd seen in over a hundred years. The traffic and noise billowed around her like curtains in the wind. She didn't care about the noise, the movement, or the people. All she cared about was the builder; her love; her best friend.

She had picked the city square to begin her search. Shops of various kinds lined the sidewalks in all four directions. She would stand there for as long as it took. If it were years, she didn't mind. She was going to find Truss.

"Come on, it's this way," a rasping voice said. Ruth turned to see who had spoken the words. They had a distinct ring. They were not like the muffled noise of pedestrians. She could hear all the typical sounds of the physical world, but it was like listening through a waterfall. This voice had been crisp as if it came from the same dimension she was occupying.

With a half spin, she spotted him at once. No, not him. Them. Two large boulder-like figures. The lines of their bodies bulged and curled in unnatural ways. Their exposed skin looked like it had been burned, scarred. They were the most frightful sight Ruth had ever beheld. They were the embodiment of the word, monster.

One wore a dark cloak covered in tears and filth. The other mongrel-looking character was smaller but only had on ripped trousers. Each of them had one end of a piece of chain they dragged noisily along the concrete. They looked like they could have been castaways from a ship that came directly from hell.

She crouched down and watched them as they passed. They were certainly two of the Molgothrian hoard. These were the bound ones whom Councilor Atromus had warned her of. They emitted that familiar half-glow; they were sub-materialized. She was now part of their realm. She had been in a different phase of the spectrum thus far. It scared her to realize that she, too, would be visible to these goons of Molgothra. She choked back a gasp when it occurred to her that Truss would be exposed as well.

"I saw it right around this corner," The larger bulging one said to the other. She thought the smaller one looked very much like a rat with its big ears and rodent-like face. She stepped quietly toward a nearby bench. She needed to hide. It would be bad to let them see her.

"I don't believe you. Are you sure your eye isn't playing a trick?" The ratty one hissed. The boulder-looking one was about to respond, but he stopped when the chain caught on the corner of the street curb. It jerked out of the ratty one's hand and clambered to the pavement. He looked up at the boulder-like freak. "You knuckle-dragging snot rocket. Watch where you're leading the chain."

"It's not my fault you dropped the chain. I'm still holding my end," The Walking Boulder said. His companion spun and looked around as if there should be someone else to witness the stupidity. Ruth crouched lower and peered through the slats of the bench at the two gremlins.

Rat reached out with an arm that looked too long for his body. He smacked Boulder across the face. He had apparently had enough. Now he dropped his end of the chain and returned the blow. They stood their trading punches until it escalated into a noisy brawl. The two swung and bit like a pair of wild animals. Ruth would have found it funny if they weren't so frightening.

"Oh, wait. It's coming," Rat said. Boulder swung once more and landed a mighty blow across his little friend's back. After tumbling forward, he maneuvered back on his feet. "Stop it already, you jabber giant."

Boulder stood dumb. He either couldn't remember what they were there for, or he hadn't known in the first place.

"What's coming?" Boulder asked.

"This was your idea, don't you remember?" Rat barked.

"Oh right, the man-thing."

"That's right. And what are we going to do to the man-thing?" Rat asked as if he were speaking to a child who'd bumped his head.

"We could trap it," Boulder said with a triumphant noise. He reached for the chain next to his ankle, as did Rat.

"That's right, you dim wit. It's coming, let's hide over there," Rat said. They lifted the chain this time. Although not completely quite, they did manage to duck behind the corner of a nearby building. Ruth turned in the direction they cast their expectant gaze.

A man rounded the corner. It looked like a human. She adjusted her glasses. It was a human. She was certain. It didn't have the glow of sub-materialization. She watched the human zip along the sidewalk, not knowing why the two brutes would care. Could they be so stupid, she wondered. Their chain would have no effect on a mortal. It was not made of corporeal material. Even she could see that from fifty paces away.

At once, she realized it was not the human that Boulder and Rat were after. It was the one following behind. She nearly jumped up when she saw him. She could have run to him. She could have screamed his name. She longed to come out of hiding and run to her love, Truss.

He was shadowing the human as they walked along the sidewalk. His eyes were locked in deep concentration. Truss had his sketchbook in hand and was making copious notes. Ruth's heart could have burst as she watched. Just to see him was a treat. She could have watched him walk for ages.

Wait, she thought. He won't know me. He might think I'm an enemy. If I scream, I'll reveal my position to the Rat and Boulder. What do I do? She stayed in her crouched position for another second. It was nearly a second too long. Her indecision was going to get Truss trapped.

Just as she was about to stand and take her chances, the human took a left turn. He dissipated into a shop located along the sidewalk. Truss paused for a split second, looked up at the sign, drew a quick sketch and then followed the human into the store. Ruth sighed. This would buy her a few seconds she hoped.

"Where did he go?" Boulder said far too loudly.

"He ducked into that building. Now shut up. We'll nab him when he comes out."

Ruth was biting her nails. Truss wouldn't know what to do. Her mistake had left him vulnerable. It was her fault he was in this mess. Ruth tightened the straps of her backpack, took a deep breath, and stood. She was going to shout at the two bumbling monsters, but her voice wouldn't cooperate.

Instead, she stepped forward, not quite sure what she was going to do. Her feet betrayed her. Clumsy as mud, she tripped. The contents of her backpack rattled, and she grunted at the poor footing. She caught herself before falling, but the two gremlins also caught sight of her.

"Hey, look," Rat said. "It's another man-thing." He pointed in her direction.

"No, it's not. It's smaller," Boulder argued. They studied her with their dull, unintelligent eyes. She felt like she'd been trapped in the stare of a pair of feral predators.

"Hey, fellas. Don't mind me." She said with an awkward wave. They continued their conversation, ignoring her greeting.

"It doesn't matter if it's smaller, let's catch it. Might make for good eating." Rat said.

She saw providence in it as she began to run. Her legs pumped like firing pistons. She knew she could transport to a safe location with ease, but this was better. She would lead them away from Truss. Hopefully, she could lose the two idiots and jump back to the spot. It was difficult leaving Truss behind. She wanted to go to him, but she knew this was for the best.

The chain clanged against everything they dragged it across. She could hear the goons' rasping voices arguing with each other as she sped away. Once or twice, she slowed so that they would feel like there was a chance of catching her. Although it was clear, these two baboons were useless.

She had run twenty-five blocks before she was certain she had lost them. It was possible they could follow her scent, so she kept running. She planned to lead them out of town before she doubled back. She didn't know much about how the bound ones worked, but evading them was easy. In fact, it bothered her how easy it was. She had heard many stories about the Molgothrians, but they never ended like this.

TO BUILD

THE ENORMOUS STRUCTURE WAS fascinating to The Observer. He had wandered into the tallest man-made building he had so far seen on this planet. Its uniform shape and sharp silhouette begged him to take a closer look.

For many hours he watched the people doing many different things. There was some type of dress code judging by the similarity in apparel. Glancing down at his own outfit he realized how different he would appear if he were not invisible.

He stood motionless in a bank of cubicles for a time. The people busied themselves with various tasks. It reminded him of a lively ant bed after a rain storm. The activity mesmerized him. After observing for a few hours, he began to write in his sketchbook.

"I've discovered something new. I had previously thought that the LBBs only enjoyed carrying things. I can see now

that they enjoy other pastimes. I'm standing in a room of LBBs attached to lifeless illuminated panels. They stare for hours at a time, pushing a small device on a flat surface. Information with various shades of unimportance jumps across their screens. Yet their attention remains fixed."

He glanced around the cubicle jungle he stood within, and then out through the windows. The scenic view allowed him to see the entire city stretched out in every direction. He turned his attention back to his notebook.

"The structure these LBBs occupy is an engineering marvel. It reaches into the sky as if it will scrape the sun and moon on their passage. It is a feat of enormous grandeur. How proud must be the builder..."

Something in that last line gave him pause. He stared at the word builder where his pencil had stopped. It was familiar and yet distant. He continued to write.

"The LBBs have limited strength and a forced schedule of eating and sleeping. Despite this, they have managed great things."

He had more to write, but his pencil stopped once more. He realized it was not only the building that had caught his imagination. It was the builder of this impressive skyscraper that he wanted to understand. It was not just curiosity, he began to see. It was envy. He had spent so many years only observing that he wondered. In huge letters, he wrote once more.

"Could I build a building like this?"

The Observer looked around and considered its design. He noticed the lack of vegetation within this enormous skyscraper. It was something of a cramped aquarium. The air was a little stale, and the space was inefficient. He imagined how he would have designed the building if it were his task to do so. It was a novel thought.

With a spark of creativity, he buried himself in his notebook. He turned to the next empty page and began to draw. In the forty thousand-plus days he had spent in this biosphere, he never drew without reference. Every sketch in all the countless books he had filled were things found. This was completely different.

His hand mimicked the speed of his mind. It moved so fast his eyes strained to keep up with the shape that was forming on the page. It was like a bolt of lightning had struck. In a flash, he saw a formed structure where the LBBs could work. It had similarities to the place where he was standing. However, in this theoretical design, each floor could open to the air.

As the building took form on the page, he designated outcroppings for hanging gardens. Once he had the macro structure drawn, he turned the page. He began on a schematic for an efficient airflow system. It would use the gardens to keep the air fresh. He integrated the water systems into a garden that run up the center of the building's interior.

Like the climax of a fireworks display, his mind was exploding with a battery of images. He saw complex structures, and a second later, they materialized on the page by his own hand. The building was symbiotic. It would be a living thing. Charts and diagrams emerged on the paper before him. He visualized a rotating foundation. It would ensure that the view was always changing.

It took 89 pages to contain the vision he had just experienced. His pencil finally came to rest. He imagined himself building it. He could feel the sense of accomplishment welling up. He had just created something, and it had produced an incredible rush of emotion. The sentiment lasted a few brief moments. He relished the feeling of victory as he visualized his building. A cloud of serenity rested on him for another second before it was driven away.

Like a tidal wave, it hit him. A deep feeling of loss pushed away his silver lining. The joy he had just experienced was empty. A darkness hung over him in the loss.

"I'm Trapped," He said aloud. Although, the ants in their cubicles did not hear.

Questions had slept in his subconscious for years. They awoke like angry creatures within his consciousness.

"What is my purpose?" He let the question sit for a long moment as he considered it. "I want to build something." He knew he could not have satisfaction. He was the observer. It's all he had ever known. All around him, the human ants were experiencing satisfaction with their witless tasks. He was jealous of their simplicity.

THE VISION

THE OBSERVER ATTEMPTED TO quiet his mind. It was rushing with a race of negativity and scorn. He had nothing to direct his ill will toward, but his intense frustration was beginning to boil. He was oscillating through an entire gamut of emotions that he was not aware he possessed.

A young man in business attire was approaching a nearby cubicle. He was dressed in a well-fitted suit. His hair was tight and clean. His shoes looked like two black mirrors. The man wore a blue tie with a precise knot at the point where his neck met his shirt. A subtle pinstripe was set at a slight contrast to the otherwise black fabric of his blazer.

The cubicle was his domain. Without hesitation, he entered with an effortless gait and made to sit. He sat for a brief moment, but the chair could hardly contain his exuberance. He stood once more and looked around the room above the cubicles.

The Observer had been too occupied to notice, but the floor was almost entirely empty of its workers. Outside the wall of windows, he could see that the sun was setting in the west. He began to think about how he might spend the dark hours of the night. He often enjoyed...

"Goodbye cubicle 6, It was nice knowing you." The young man's words interrupted the observer's thoughts. The observer trained his attention on the business man.

Had he heard correctly? This man had just spoken to the inanimate objects around him. He pulled out his book and pencil, turned past his latest pages, and began sketching the man.

Before the drawing was complete, the man stood and walked toward the exit. The Observer followed with fascination. He was happy to be distracted from his dark mood. He was enthralled once more.

From the back seat of the man's car, The Observer studied him. He felt confident that he had learned the answer to at least one of his questions about humans.

"The LBBs are not able to teleport. They have not yet discovered space-time jumping. Their locomotive capabilities are limited to these ridiculous fuel-burning carriages."

He let his pencil catalog empirical data about the vehicle's physics, trajectory, and mass. These types of equations he could allow his subconscious to handle. The real mystery was behind the steering wheel.

The roads were busy, but the drive was uneventful. He enjoyed the bump and jitter of the car ride. He had not expected it to be soothing, but he determined that he would like to ride in cars more often. He made a few more sketches of the young man.

When the man pulled his car into a suburban driveway, the Observer wished the drive had been longer. The young man got out of the car and skipped into another smaller building. The observer assumed it was some type of home. From the back seat, he teleported himself into the home.

The house was warm and lived in. It had inviting incandescent lights and plenty of artistic decoration. This was his first time to see a human dwelling place. In other circumstances, he would have liked to browse around a little. However, a second after porting into the house the man passed through the room.

"Hey, I'm home." He said with sadness in his voice. The Observer followed him as he moved through the house. They came to a bright room where a female was preparing terrestrial food.

"Hey Honey, how did it go?" The woman said with compassion. Her husband looked down at the floor as if ashamed. The pain on his face was a surprise to The

Observer. He turned the page in his book and began taking notes. The woman continued, "Oh, it's ok, Honey, we knew it wasn't a sure thing."

She moved in close to embrace him. As she wrapped her arms around him, he deflated further. He had appeared fine while at work. Even in the car, his mood had been healthy. The Observer doubted his observational skills. How could he have missed this? The man broke the act and burst with a loud proclamation.

"I'm just kidding! I got the promotion!" He wrapped his arms around his wife. This time, rather than a simple hug, he picked her up off the ground and spun her around. "It was unbelievable. They only interviewed the others as a formality! It was always going to be me!"

"Are you serious? That's great!" She said as he put her back on the ground. "I'm so proud of you." She kissed him and held onto him as he continued to talk.

"It seriously hasn't sunk in yet. I just can't believe it's finally happening. As of an hour ago, I am no longer a systems analyst. I'm finally going to get to make something. Ever since I was young, I knew this is what I was supposed to be doing."

The Observer lifted his hand and snapped his fingers. The scene froze. The river of time was too much. He needed to find land. His emotions were almost like a living thing, and he could hardly make sense of them. It fascinated him while filling him with a great sense of loss at his own dissatisfaction.

He wanted to feel what this man was feeling. The Observer wanted to know his own purpose. Not knowing what else to do, he retreated into the pages of his book. He began to draw the frozen scene in front of him. Within a few seconds, a face emerged on the page. Another second and the entire scene existed in pencil lead.

The Observer raised his hand in the air and slowly made a circular motion with his fingertip. As if it were a simple machine, the entire scene reversed slowly. With another gesture, the scene replayed as the man once again said, "I knew this is what I was supposed to be doing."

NEAR

RUTH ROAMED. THE EVENING was cool and crisp as the warm night air gave way to the cooler night temperatures. The city had calmed from its manic frenzy now that night had come. She had her backpack pulled tight and her hair tied back in a tight bun.

She had evaded the two goons, that she had affectionately named Rat and Boulder. Still, knowing that they, and more of their kind, were out there kept her vigilant. Her search for Truss had become more complicated with every step. Now she had to consider her own safety and worry about monsters finding her beloved.

She had been walking the downtown area for a few hours. Her single sighting of Truss had been something she could not repeat. After returning to the shop that he had entered, she hoped to find him. By the time she arrived, he was long gone. Despite the missed opportunity, she felt hopeful that she would see him again soon. Her faith in the King and all things good drove her forward.

She wondered what he might be doing at that moment. She was confident that he was still within the city limits. She had spent a significant amount of time in cities of all different kinds on this world and others. She was not distracted by the movement and busyness.

A concrete pail sidewalk stretched out in front of her. There were fewer people out on the streets now that it was dark. Yet some late walkers populated the city byways. She followed the foot traffic, being careful not to come in contact with pedestrians. It was not a direct rule, but generally, she knew better than to interfere with the natives.

There was a darker reason she now avoided touching the humans. After all, it was the moment she touched a human that all her trouble had begun. Her colossal mistake was just that, a simple touch. She had intended it for good, but she should have known better. She did know better. That's what made it so awful. She knew there would be consequences to come. She knew she would pay for her mistake. Pushing it from her mind, she took a deep breath and again forced herself to focus on the task at hand.

SPOON

RUTH HAD SET HER pace to match the movement of the sidewalk traffic. So she was surprised when she nearly ran into the person in front of her. She had not been paying strict attention. Though a second earlier, she had plenty of distance between her and the other woman.

"Oh no you don't," She said as she danced out of the way, narrowly missing the human.

She started to walk again but noticed the peculiar scene. Out of the corner of her eye, she noticed the incredible stillness of the woman she had almost collided with. What caught Ruth's attention was the shape of the wrinkles in her blouse. She was like a masterful sculpture. There was no movement whatsoever. The woman had been frozen in time.

"Spoon!" She shouted with excitement. She had been enamored with silverware since she had arrived on Earth. She had often used the word. "I've got you now."

Ruth looked around with new hope in her eyes. The entire city scene was still as stone, but only for a second. As she watched the cityscape moved in reverse as if someone had hit rewind. It paused and then after a brief moment played the previous 3 seconds. It could mean only one thing. She had found a clue.

Kneeling, she pulled her pack from her back. In one fluid motion, she had it open and laying in front of her on the sidewalk pavement.

In another fraction of a second, she produced the map from the pack. This map had a similar look to the one that had been sprawled out on her desk. However, it was only a map of the city. A smaller pocket in the pack contained her quill and inkwell. These she laid out on the ground, uncapped, and prepared to write. Now poised for marking, she closed her eyes and concentrated.

Truss's time stream was tied to hers. Their distance apart did not matter. If he paused, regressed, or warped time, she could feel it. She could roughly estimate the direction from which a time warp originated. It was hard to visualize it and not precise. Truss had trained her to see it like ripples in time that flow from one direction. She went through the meditation process, hoping her excitement would not ruin her accuracy. She tried to still the chatter in her mind.

She began to get a sense of it. It seemed to touch her first somewhere near her right shoulder blade. She opened one eye and peeked at her surroundings. That would mean that her builder was somewhere northeast of her.

She opened her eyes. Excitement blazed. She dipped her quill in the inkwell, tapped it on the edge, and penned a solid X in rich red ink. She then drew a small arrow pointing in a northeasterly direction.

With another burst of speed, she capped her inkwell, flicked the ink off her quill, rolled the map. She returned the contents to her bag. Within another second she had the pack on her back, and she was heading North East.

WATCHING

THE INVISIBLE OBSERVER GAZED at the couple in the kitchen. They were still frozen and motionless, but certainly not without life. Chiseled into their still faces was the hope and excitement of a new adventure. They were happy to be alive. As he watched, he thought that even these two, frozen as they are in this infinite moment, have more life pouring out of them and into them than he had experienced in an entire century here.

With a gesture, he let the scene play out. The couple became increasingly giddy as they continued to talk. For the observer, the joy of the moment was like alcohol in a wound. The bitter taste of jealousy filled him as he put his pencil behind his ear.

Ploddingly, he found his way out of the house. Passing through the front door invisibly, he stood on the front lawn.

The vitality of the city's daytime had given way to darkness, and now, what had earlier seemed to be an attractive landscape for observation was nothing more than a palpable reminder of his own lack of meaning. There was no visible moon to sing down its mild melody of light. The night sounds were so different here in the city. A distant road roared like a river, and the squeak of a passing car's brakes made for a poor imitation of bird songs. The orange buzzing glow of a street light painted his world in monochromatic tedium, unlike the beautiful full-spectrum sunbeams that the moon often provided.

How do I quit? He thought with a dark tone. He thought that maybe this was some type of punishment. Maybe he was once like the creatures he observed. What evil he would have to do to earn this prison. He corrected himself. It has not all been bad.

He captured his thoughts. This was not like him to think such dark things. He decided to return to his peaceful place for a time of reflection.

Restoring his book to his front pocket, he closed his eyes, took a deep breath, and vanished. In his downtrodden state, he had forgotten to place a hand on his felt top hat.

Without a body below it to keep it aloft, the hat tumbled lifelessly to the ground, hit the edge of the sidewalk where he had been standing with a thud, and rolled shortly before coming to a stop.

That's where it would have sat indefinitely like so many other pieces of debris trapped between two dimensions; Not fully materialized for terrestrial observation but abandoned by their owners. Earthly beings were designed to be aware of such a thin spectrum of the electromagnetic field. The non-terrestrial regions of the universe were so vast that an abandoned top hat was theoretically non-existent in the cosmic sense. That is, at least, how it would have been if it remained abandoned.

LOST

RUTH FELT LOST. SHE had followed the best that she could, the direction in which she thought the time warp had come from. Every few blocks she had pulled her map out of her pack and studied it.

It was always hard to tell how far away a space-time warp had taken place. There were always unknown variables to be considered. She thought at first that it must have been within walking distance but after a few hours of walking, she was beginning to doubt her original sense.

As she moved Northeast the city blocks with high-rise buildings had given way to a less clustered scene of industrial complexes. Traversing that territory for still longer the landscape changed further into suburban housing establishments.

Ruth felt sure that this would be a fruitless journey. She considered the numerous neighborhoods that she would have to traverse. What if he was in a house? There seemed no way to check everyone. Her disheartening was growing with every further step.

Sometimes, as she began to work her way through the suburbs, she had to climb a fence, circumvent an automobile, or otherwise avoid obstacles. It felt strange to her to be so tied to the standard form of terrestrial locomotion. She usually would phase through obstacles as if she were nothing more than a ghost, but she needed to stay materialized to be sure she didn't miss any other time-space disruptions.

There was some joy in the walking. She had rarely, if ever, walked such a stretch on this planet without phasing or jumping to another region. Being so single-minded was therapeutic. It had been a long time since she felt that she had a substantive clue about her mission.

Three hours and forty-seven minutes found Ruth in a neighborhood that looked quite like every other one she had thus far traveled through. It was night, even though it was well lit by the tireless street lights. It came into her mind that a check of the map was in order.

She paused in the middle of an intersection. The hour of the morning that it was meant there was little movement, and almost no city sounds in the distance. The sibling houses spread out at consistent intervals along the road.

With a practiced motion, she reached around to the pack on her back and pulled the rolled-up map from it.

Unrolling it in the air before her face, she began to study. She had covered a substantial portion of the map. Within another quarter hour of walking, she would be out of the city. She considered how strictly she could rely on Atromus' comment. She felt that although she had been following a solid clue, it was turning out to be a dead end. Doubling back and walking the same line seemed to be the only option. Maybe if she strayed from the map line more liberally, this time, she could find another clue.

The stillness of the early morning was a ready canvas for what happened next. A tingle of electricity momentarily touched her at the edges of her body. It was light and almost imperceptible. At the same moment, a block of houses away, a sharp light erupted into the sky. It flashed quickly, silhouetting the neighborhood in front of her.

With one fluid motion, she rolled and returned the map to her bag as she began to sprint down the length of the street. It was impossible at this distance with a time-space jump to tell if someone was arriving or departing since both ends of a temporary wormhole were identical. However, she knew that her best chance of finding the treasure of her search was at the epicenter of that flash.

She pumped with excitement. Anytime she had ever needed to be somewhere quickly, she would simply leap there. It took all her mental strength not to. Houses blurred by as she moved at an inhuman speed. Her feet lightly caressed the pavement as she rocketed forward.

She abruptly stopped as she came to the point at which she thought she perceived the time-space blast. Again, there was stillness. The orange buzz of a streetlight was the only sound that invaded the silence. Motionless, she listened and watched for movement. A long moment told her that there was none.

She began to spin, looking for signs of him. Slowly, she turned, trying to pay attention to every detail. All of these houses looked so much the same it seemed ridiculous to imagine that she'd see anything different when looking from one yard to another. After surveying the immediate area for three full spins, she again pulled out her map. This time, she knelt down as she pulled out her inkwell and quill. She quickly marked the location of the map with a rich red X. After staring for a few seconds, she circled it and stood after putting it all back in her bag.

She had found a bigger clue than the last but had almost no idea what to do. The gravity of the moment pressed on her with an overwhelming weight. For a long time, she stood in the street thinking about the next step.

With hardly a conscious thought, she decided to survey the four houses in the immediate area. She had to be close. This was where the flash had happened. A slow, methodical pace carried her to the nearest of the four houses. There were no cars in the driveway and little else of interest.

The next home investigation was also uneventful. There was a kid's colorful plastic trike next to the front door of this one. This had nothing to do with a builder so she moved on.

She was crossing the street to look at the third house when she saw it. It was velveted hope in the shape of a man's top hat. She approached slowly as the speed of her breath increased. She tried to keep her excitement in check by reminding herself that it was dark, and she could be mistaken. She became more confident in her hypothesis with every step. She began to recognize that it had the distinct shimmer of a submaterialized object as she got closer to the hat.

Standing over it, she knew exactly to whom the beautiful hat belonged. Her emotions were coming in at light speed now. The joy of finding a great clue filled her. As soon as that thought had arrived, like a box car train, it was rammed out of the station by a bigger freight car that followed. Why would he leave his hat? Was he hurt? Or naked?

Her mind raced as she began to look around. Nothing in the immediate area gave her any information on the abandoned object. She reached down and picked it up. Holding it in her hands brought back a century-old memory.

She was standing in front of him before they jumped to Earth. She placed the hat on his head. He smiled and hugged her. She knew she would be watching him from a distance, so it was not bitter. He put his entire life in her hands that day. She never dreamed that she would be in this situation, having to try to put back together the broken pieces of such a cosmic mess.

She returned to the present in her mind, but now her hands shook ever so slightly. She gazed at the hat, trying to imagine what to do next.

HATCH

A BLAND ROOM PAINTED with an uncreative shade of white was full of cafeteria-style tables and numerous people in blue hospital-issue outfits. The low, undulating murmur of a crowd bounced around in the room, commingled with the sound of lunch trays and eating. Possibly due to the uncommon level of psychotropic drugs in this particular group of people, the scene was calm.

Like most days, a line had formed at the entrance to the buffet-style food island. Most could be classified as less than excited about eating. The standard form of medication at this facility did an adequate job of pacifying the occupants but had the unfortunate side effect of almost completely eliminating the patients' appetites. The inhabitants of Shady Oak knew, however, that the medicine that they would be forced to ingest after lunch would make them intensely nauseous on an empty stomach. So they ate.

James, who was more chipper than most, sat at a table close to the exit. His tray of food had a colorful spread of macaroni and cheese, a Styrofoam cup of broccoli, and a cardboard milk carton. Tucked tightly into his left hand was a matching set of plastic silverware. Metal objects, especially ones with sharp edges, were strictly prohibited. A crumpled paper towel was gripped mercilessly in his other hand.

An absent smile was painted across James' face, and he was humming a tune. It had been plaguing him most of the morning. Waking up with a tune but being too drugged to identify it was one of the most annoying things possible. He paused and gripped the fork, knife, and spoon harder. Through closed teeth and with a little more volume, he buzzed out the 5 note melody again.

"Beetlejuice!" a voice erupted from across the table. James didn't noticed anyone sit down. He looked up to see Riley in the opposing seat.

Riley was friendly but had dull eyes. He had incredibly dark complexion even for a black man. Riley was probably in his early sixties and was greying around the edges of his tight curly hair. James knew Riley well, since they had been sharing a room for almost two years now.

He had gotten used to Riley's inability to control his incessant blurting. Dr. Thomas had explained to James that he would be responsible to help Riley when needed. It was a program to help James and others with higher level functionality to feel valued and to ensure continued recovery. James, like many others, was utterly convinced of his own sanity, but he welcomed the responsibilities he had with his roommate.

Riley, because he had brain damage to the frontal lobe, was inhibited from being anything but blunt and often off topic. Because of this, it was normally Riley that set the topic of conversation, but this time James had a tune mystery that needed to be cracked.

"Beetlejuice," Riley reiterated a little too loudly. Riley was not on the psychotropic drugs that many of the other patients were so his blurting was in jagged contrast to the rounded sounds of the room. "You're singing Beetlejuice right?"

"That's a movie, not a song." James smiled as he softly replied. Riley grunted and dug into his tray which was much more sloppily arranged. After watching him a moment James spoke up, "Napkin?"

Riley looked up with macaroni smeared around the edges of his lips. After a long moment of silence, he spoke with a full mouth of food. The cheesy mixture smacked as he said, "That ain't no song either crap-shoes."

James was used to being called strange names, so rather than reply, he reached across the table with his napkin and held it out to Riley. He accepted, wiped his mouth, and again fixed his attention to the food tray.

A light came across James' face. "It's the song the aliens played in Close Encounters." It was as if he had just been released from a heavy burden. He opened his hand with the silverware and began to eat, and imagined the scene in the movie where the extraterrestrial ships arrived over the mountain. He had been a young boy when he'd first seen the film, but was endlessly fascinated by the potential for extraterrestrials. The movie held a heightened sense of meaning to him ever since he had learned of his own cosmic importance.

He continued to eat as he said, "So silly to think that an advanced race would use linear travel to cross even some-thing as small as a galaxy. They would have had to start the journey long before the human race even existed."

"You too fat to fit in a spaceship, plump-rump." Riley paused only a second and laughed to himself at his comment. A moment later, James joined in the laughter.

With a chuckle, he responded, "What, this little ole' thing?" He leaned over as if to look down at his butt. Riley reached out his hand, pointed his finger in James' face, and blurted loudly enough for everyone to hear.

"plump-rump, plump-rump, plump-rump!" The entire room got quiet and looked in their direction. A thick moment of silence accompanied the stares. The entire cafeteria erupted in laughter. Repeated echoes of Riley's words bounced around the room.

James was no stranger to this game. He pushed his chair back from the table, stood up, and climbed up onto the chair so that he was a full body length taller than the seated lunchroom. Now that everyone could see him, he bent over slightly and put his rear on display. He turned for everyone to get a good look at the literal butt of Riley's joke. This crowd was so eager for a laugh, and it was better to embrace the mocking and give everyone the gift of some fun. It actually made him feel good to bring some laughter to the room, even if it was at the expense of his own self-image.

As the laughter began to die down, James got down off the chair. The too-late shouts of an orderly could be heard over the murmur of laughter. James returned to his seat across from Riley. Riley was still giggling at the hilarity he had just created, and James laughed lightly to himself, mostly out of pride for diffusing such a potentially embarrassing situation.

"Luckily, I don't have to try and fit my butt into a spaceship I can just visualize where I want to be and..." He trailed off as he thought about how his last attempt at a time-space jump had gone terribly wrong. No, not terribly wrong. Terribly wrong would be getting stranded at an accidental intersection of a massive gravity well and his own temporary wormhole. The worst that had happened was Dr. Thomas' conclusions of insanity were reinforced. That was nothing new.

Clarity seemed to come to his eyes as he reasoned this out. Maybe the reason he was not able to leap was because he was rusty. It had been so many years since he had leaped that maybe he had made a mistake in his subconscious calculations. Who knows? Maybe he had mistakenly charted a path through an active star. His subconscious probably caught the mistake and simply aborted the jump.

What he needed was exercise. Much like his unkempt body, his mental muscle was out of shape as well. He brimmed with joy as he began to regain his cosmic confidence. He looked up and said, "Riley, what would you think about taking a trip out of here?"

Riley pondered this for a long moment. He then said thoughtfully, "I'll go If you'll take me to Hooters, Captain Kirk."

VISITOR

THE LIVING ROOM WAS dim as the sporadic light of a television danced across the walls. The sounds of some poorly written crime drama played out on the oversized screen.

The old sunken couch was upholstered with a knit floral pattern. It was old and sunken. The two humans on the couch, a man and a woman, sat at either end. Both were unaware that someone sat between them.

The Observer was tired. At least that is the best way to describe how he felt. His body had endless energy, but his motivation was another matter all together. His insatiable urge to observe was still present. However, at that moment he had taken up the television as an alternative pastime. The programing was not interesting to him.

He sat, an invisible intruder, sandwiched between two unaware humans. The TV spat its criminal justice jargon at the three disconnected individuals. Although he stared forward, he wandered the dark caves in his mind. He was trying to remember something, anything from before his arrival. There had to be something from before. No matter how hard he pressed, he could not dig up a memory. He had arrived with an empty mind. Everything but his operating system had been removed from his brain.

The last few days, he had learned more about the humans than he had learned about any species in decades. They were so conflicted and complex. They seem twisted and bent. He got glimpses of the original design for humanity. It was magnificent and beautiful, but it was warped at the same time. The splendor that could be humanity did not remain. He wondered if he were as bent as these mortals. He wondered if that was why he had no memory from before his arrival.

It was pity he felt most for this race. He glanced at the two humans on either side of him, who were obviously mates. They were magnificent creatures with immeasurable talent. Yet here they sat doing something so insipid. They shared nothing more than a cheap, fabricated experience. Television, what an artificial medium. What had happened in the history of this race that twisted their ambitions and purpose? Where did their design come from, and how did these creatures become so bent?

The woman on his right suddenly got up. A moment later the man extended his hand and pressed the power button on the television remote. He then followed the woman out of the room. Now alone in the darkness The Observer' mind began to wander.

He thought through a list of observations he had made prior to reaching the city. Nothing interested him there. He thought about the street creep who tried to steal the woman's handbag. He idly wondered what the young man was doing now. This train of thought bored him.

He closed his eyes and stilled his mind. The voice in his head quieted to a whisper and then went silent.

Silence surrounded him.

Stillness enveloped him.

An explosion of light surrounded him. He was not altogether sure what was happening. Was this a dream? Had he accidentally teleported? The vision before him had the illusory glow of the imaginary. Yet it looked real. The room and couch faded as the scene gained clarity. For a brief moment, he felt serenity.

He was looking out over a vast expanse of space. Stars and galaxies sang their songs of light in the distance. His body floated. The nothing caressed his skin. He found its cold reaches comforting somehow. The blinding brightness of a medium dwarf star assaulted his eyes, but he could not look away. He floated motionless in open space as he watched the scene before him.

His body was experiencing the sensation of weightlessness. Something caught his attention from below. He looked in the direction of his feet and saw the most beautiful orb of green. An enormous world crawled upward in its orbit. He watched with passionate interest as the planet crept upward to fill his entire view. He could hear the green world serenading softly as it inched by. Its rhythms and patterns hummed melodic notes as it passed.

He lost himself in the vision as it moved in his direction. Warm starlight brushed the upper crest of the planet's horizon. An amber glow illuminated the outer rim of the world as the light excited its edges.

The visionary planet had no oceans. Large pools of clear water dotted the forest floor. He could see deep into the blue depths. The jungled wilds of the planet wrapped around the world like a green blanket.

"Where am I?" He turned to the stars that were visible around him in the expanse. He looked for a familiar constellation. There were none that he recognized.

He watched with delight as the planet began to rotate. The green canopy hugged the horizon under the amber atmosphere. It was a magical procession.

The emerald sphere moved forward with purpose as the lower half faded away into shadow. He watched the vision evolve for ages. There was something on the approaching side of the planet. His pulse increased with anxiety. He stopped breathing as he waited.

Out of the flare of a star beam, the silhouette of a magnificent mountain began to take shape. The spinning world presented its greatest feature for him to behold.

It was as if time itself slowed when the mountain was in full view. He felt the gravity of its enormous peaks. Each crag and jut was a world unto itself. The astronomical enormity of the mountain filled his entire mind. It was a world's worth of rock and dirt in each of its many peaks.

The tops of the mountain peaks were not covered in snow. Where the atmosphere got too thin, the vegetation simply stopped. Yet, the rock faces of the mountain continued on far past. The spires of rock stretched heavenward like cathedrals in the sky. As he watched the rotation of the green world, the mountain moved ever closer.

The green world continued to turn. He was many kilometers above the surface of the planet, but he was on a collision course with the mountain.

The mountain approach, he realized that the upper peaks of the mountain were detached. In fact, they floated like an field of asteroids above the mountaintop.

He awaited his collision with the mountain as something desirable. He waited with baited breath to touch down on the mountain's floating heights. His entire body was alive with anticipation.

***

"You always do this," a woman's voice said. It was angry and acidic. The voice did not fit the vision. He was roused from intoxicating images with a start. The Observer opened his eyes and realized he was still in the living room.

How long had he been there? It must have been all night because sunlight was shining in the windows in the adjacent dining area. The morning rays glazed the room in orange light. The woman's voice came again, "Just because you don't yell doesn't mean you aren't mean."

He looked back to see the couple standing in the hallway. They fired angry looks like mortar shells. The voices continued behind him. The woman yelled, and the man responded quietly, which seemed to anger her more.

The Observer felt as if some fresh air was in order. A flash enveloped the room and this invisible house guest was gone.

ESCAPE

JAMES AND RILEY WERE madly packing the entirety of their belongings into a stolen trash bag. Riley stood at the ready with the gaping mouth of the bag in hand as James quickly tucked the few gathered contents he could find into it. Among the accouterments he had acquired were extra scrubs, both of their toothbrushes, and six cardboard cartons of milk Riley had stolen at lunch.

"Those'll go stinky," Riley said as he gestured toward the milk cartons, "like yo breath!" he added with a smile of delight at his own cleverness. James smiled back but let it fade from his face as he responded.

"I know, but we don't have any other food. We should be long gone before they go bad. I just wish we had some beef jerky." James took the bag from Riley and tied a loose knot in the top as he thought of what he was about to attempt. He admitted to himself that he was nervous. Maybe it was as Dr. Thomas had said. Maybe he was crazy. James had rarely ever actually entertained the notion of his own insanity. He had told Dr. Thomas when he first arrived, "If knowing what I know now makes me crazy, then I don't want to be sane."

Riley wrenched the bag from James' hands aggressively. "I'll carry da hobo sack." He said with a tone of agitation in his voice.

"Have I ever told you how I discovered my cosmic importance?" James asked as he sat on the bed. It creaked as James' generous weight stressed its structure. The pale room had two single beds parallel to either side of a window with exterior bars. Riley shook his head as he sat down on the other bed. Riley's more aged frame, being less voluminous, made no sound as he landed ungracefully on the thin, uncomfortable mattress.

James continued. "Growing up, I was always the 'big kid' at school." James put his fingers in the air to symbolize air quotes.

"Still are!" Riley said injudiciously.

"You're right, I still am, but it doesn't bother me now that I know who I really am." The old metal bed groaned as James adjusted his position. "I never really fit in wherever I went." He looked at the floor, remembering those hard days. "My parents died in a car wreck when I was pretty young, and I became the ward of the state."

"Di'jya get a foster family?" Riley blurted.

"Yes, I...in fact, I got seven foster families. None of them were really bad, but I just never fit in. I always felt like I was an inconvenience." He leaned back against his pillow as he continued. "When I was eighteen, I got out on my own and started working at a grocery store. I even had a girlfriend named Laura."

"Plump-Rump had a girlfriend? D'jal get physical?" Riley said as he dropped the bag and rubbed his chest as if he felt aroused.

"Yeah, Plump-Rump had a girlfriend, and I'm a gentleman, so..." He paused for a minute. Riley seemed somewhat deflated by the lack of details on this particular subject. James continued. "Laura's dad owned the grocery store. One afternoon, he caught us making out in the back of the storeroom."

"I knew it!" Riley blurted victoriously. James smiled.

"I still remember she had these deep green eyes. I thought she was beautiful. Apparently, her dad didn't think we were so beautiful together. He fired me and told her she couldn't see me anymore."

"I'll kick him in the guts and drop him like a toilet seat!" Riley shouted as he rose to his feet. He began to pace back and forth between the beds as James continued his story.

"We tried to continue seeing each other, but she was really uncomfortable going against her dad's wishes. Before a week had gone by, he had made plans for her to go off to college in another town." Riley's footsteps were the only sound in the room for a long moment.

"We outa find 'er so you can finish making out!" Riley said as if it were the most brilliant plan possible. He slowed and sat back on the bed, tired from his pacing.

"She got married six months later to some dude she was going to college with."

"I'll kick him dead too." Riley again blurted, but with less enthusiasm.

"No, I'm happy for her. I was nothing but trouble then, and if it wasn't for her, I wouldn't have learned about who I really am." James sat up as his excitement level grew. "See, I was in a really dark place. I had been thinking about how I'd kill myself. I decided that I would do it by taking an entire bottle of Tylenol." James swallowed hard as he recollected his decision. "I got everything set up, I even lit a candle. Right before I did it, there was like a..." James trailed off as he searched for the words.

"Yo Plump-Rump chickened out!" Riley said abruptly.

"No, it was like a shimmering light filled the room. This amazing woman was suddenly there. She was like a goddess or something. She looked like she wanted to cry. She didn't say anything, but it was like I knew she had been watching me. I couldn't do it. I knew she didn't want me to. I wasn't sure if she was just a vision or if she was real until..."

Riley cut him off again, "Until you got physical?" James laughed.

"No. Until she touched me, she placed her hand on my head, and it was like I had a total meltdown in my brain. I could suddenly see who I really was. I had thousands of years of memories that suddenly resurfaced. It was like I had been awake from a dream for 20 years but suddenly remembered it in extreme detail. I remembered that I had special powers and that I was cosmically important." Riley stared blankly. "Then she was gone."

"Did'n even getta phone numba?" Riley asked unceremoniously.

"I realized that my life up until that point had just been part of a greater, longer story. I even found out that James isn't my real name."

"Oh, da goddess told you your name was Plump-Rump?" Riley snickered, as did James.

"No, my name is actually Truss."

GUEST

THE SMELL OF MASHED potatoes and pork chops permeated the air. The large formal dining room was opulently staged to the right of the front entrance of the oversized house. The rich dark wood of the mahogany table was a nice accent where it sat below a crystal chandelier. On the cream colored walls hung a scad of family pictures framed in expensive looking wood.

A family of four sat quietly eating their dinner. A TV was on somewhere in the house because its muffled sounds played soft and distant. The lack of conversation meant that the soundscape of the room was made up of chewing noises and the inadvertent clinking of forks against dining china.

The observer sat at one of the vacant seats with the family. He was back on his old game of observation, although he was not nearly as excited about his observations as of late. The human race was so varied that one day's observations seemed to completely contradict the last's. He felt he was a long way off from unraveling the mystery that surrounded these creatures' existence. Although the family did not know it, he had joined them for this meal. He took notes and drew as they ate.

The table would seat twelve people, so for this meal, it seemed sparse even with the invisible dinner guest. The father, who was still dressed in business attire, shoveled a voluminous spoonful of potatoes into his already full mouth. He looked at his phone beneath the edge of the table as he chewed. His chewing was violent, and his attention was somewhere other than the room in which he sat. The observer's hand went to the page as he was about to draw the father in motion, but something caught his attention.

The man's son, a young male of about nine years old was watching his dad intently. The boy's eyes never left him except for a moment here and there where his father looked up to import more food into his face hole. The boy tried his best to keep up with the eating speed of his father, and therefore shoveled as much pork into his mouth as possible. The observer was about to draw the boy looking intently at his father when yet another thing caught his attention.

The boy's mother, who was at the opposite end of the table from her husband, happened to be studying her son closely. It was obvious that she was not particularly pleased with the notion of her son acting like the man that she no longer loved. She ate very little as she stared at the boy. When he piled too much food in his mouth, she would make a motion as if she were going to speak, but then would glance at her husband and look down at her plate. This cycle happened a few times, and the observer poised to draw the triadic interaction, but he noticed yet another thing.

The daughter, who was presumably only one human gestation cycle older than her brother, was watching her mother inordinately. Her intentions did not seem to be the same as the boy's. She watched sulkily through a shaft of hair that hung and covered half of her face. The observer thought he sensed some jealousy in it. The girl was a spitting image of her mother. She even held her eating utensil identically. He assumed that the parental imitation was intended to garner her mother's pride, but it was not working. Her mother was paying all of her attention to her little brother.

He gripped the pencil and tried to imagine how to illustrate such a complicated quadratic human chain of interaction. He had rarely ever tried to put to paper something so terribly abstract. He thought he might start with an image of the father. As his pencil touched the surface of his paper, an even more interesting thing occurred.

He saw movement with his peripheral vision and glanced over quickly. A woman came through the entrance of the room. She was unlike any human he had ever seen. She had the basic form and movement of a homosapien, but it was as if there was a shimmer or a glow that surrounded her. The light seemed to play differently with the surface of her skin than with everyone else in the room.

She had an attractive soft face and clothes that were very mismatched. Her dark rimmed glasses rode low on her nose and she slanted her head ever so slightly down so that she could look over the top of them. In fact, she seemed to be looking at him so he spun and looked behind to see what she might be looking at.

The family continued to eat as she strode slowly into the room. She cautiously placed herself in the seat across the table from him. He could see it now as she sat next to the boy. Although he was a young, healthy youth, she outshone him in an inexplicable way. It was as if the body that just walked into the room was the image to which all human forms were striving to be.

Her skin was smooth and perfect. Her motions were delicate but deliberate. Her eyes were deep and studious;

eyes that still seemed to be gazing at him. He again turned and looked behind him. What could this beautiful young woman be looking at, he thought. Behind was simply an unremarkable cream wall.

He turned back around in his chair to find that she had now begun to cry. It was not like the blubbering, selfish weeping that he had seen so many times among the humans. It was joy, at least that's what he thought for a brief moment. Through her tears, it still looked like she was staring at him. He thought of an experiment.

He leaned as far to the right as he possibly could while still remaining above the surface of the table. As he did, her eyes followed him. Could it have been a coincidence? He thought as he sat back upright. Her eyes again followed him the entire time. Is it possible that this woman can see me? It was completely unprecedented in all of his recorded memory.

Another moment passed with only the sounds of the family eating and the distant TV coming through the walls.

"I can't believe I've found you." Ruth said with a another tear forming in the corner of her eye. She breathed a sigh of relief and for the first time she began to feel as if it would be ok. The observer simply sat and watched her for a very long time. She determined it should be him who spoke next so she too sat in silence.

After quite a while, the family finished their dinner and left the room. Ruth and the Observer remained silently locked in a stare. Although it was almost completely unnoticed by the pair, a different person came in and took the dishes away to be cleaned. They stayed still without a word, studying each other. It wasn't until it got completely dark outside and the streetlights had begun to replace the sunlight with artificial glow that he finally broke the silence.

"I spoke nary a word in the five score and twelve revolutions of this world, come to me not in mystery, Have I been touched or are ye present in suth?" He thought the words sounded much more archaic than he had intended. He had often heard the people he observed speak and thought he could do better. So he tried again. "I haven't said a single word in one hundred and twelve years, tell me the truth, are you real or have I finally lost it?"

"I promise, you're entirely sane." She wiped her tears away, and a smile danced across her face. "I've been looking for you for years now." He felt as if he would explode. He had so many questions. She stood and said abruptly, "We need to get moving, we've wasted enough time here. I need to get you up to speed." She paused for a moment, looked at the floor, and added, "Somehow."

He adjusted himself but did not stand. Every inch of him was screaming for companionship, but he decided he must be cautious. "Look here, I don't know who you are. I'm quite pleased to be able to converse after such a long time, but you are moving a bit fast, don't you think? Should we not attempt to get a few things straightened out first? Now you seem to know me, or at least would like me to think you do, but I will need at least some show of good faith, or some proof that you may be trusted."

He impressed himself with that little speech and rightfully so. It felt good to stretch his lungs and speak for himself. He noted that he would like to do more of that in the future. He poised himself and waited for her response.

"This is how it goes, you're doing your part perfectly. At this point, normally I'd have a memory key that'd let you know I can be trusted." She slowed her pace and looked at him as she sat back down in the chair. "I don't have it anymore, though. I made a really stupid mistake, and I don't have the memory key."

"What is the nature of your familiarity with me?" He crossed his arms like he had seen humans do when being stern.

"While you're on this planet I was supposed to watch out for you." She said with shame in her voice.

"And in this type of arrangement, would it be normal for one like myself to be completely unaware of one like yourself?" He fired back quickly.

She rose from the chair with fervor. "Please come with me, we don't have time for this." She said emphatically enough to make the observer rise from his chair in response.

"I will do nothing of the kind until you satisfy the conditions I laid out. I find you to be infinitely intriguing and exceptionally hard to resist, but I really must stand on my instincts here. In the past century, I have become quite independent and have never once in that time been told where to go or what to do, so you will have to excuse me if I resist. If you can show me that you are to be trusted, then I will come with you on whatever errand you are trying to engage me in. Until then, however, I will remain an independent agent."

She turned toward the wall obviously to mask the fact that she was crying. This time it was not joy, but frustration that the tears arrived with.

"I've got proof, it's just not here. Will you come with me so I can show it to you?"

"I affirm that this is a valid and fair counterpoint, and as for a reciprocal offer, it has merit, but I know nothing of where you come from. In this instance, I propose that we meet at a neutral location. You bring the proof, and I will bring a fair mind."

"Where should we meet?" she asked abruptly with a little too much acid in her voice. Now knowing that she would not be leaving with her prize she allowed her anger to show.

"My earliest memory in this world is fond to me. I remember waking in a snowy expanse with an incredible desire to learn as much as possible about this planet. I will draw a map for you so that..."

She cut him off with frustration, "No need, I know exactly where it is because I chose it. I'll meet you there at this time tomorrow."

She stepped closer to the table and pulled her backpack from her back. She threw open the flap on the end and reached in.

"What are you doing?" He asked nervously.

"Here, you dropped your stupid hat." In one fluid motion she pulled from the pack and tossed him his top hat that he had been missing. She returned the bag to her back. A blast of light enveloped the room and she was gone.

OTHERS

HE STOOD STILL FOR quite some time, trying to re-imagine a world where there were others like himself. His mood grew dark as he passed through a forest of lonely memory. He thought about the long years spent roaming alone. Were they needless?

The room felt as if it were closing in on him. He placed the hat on his head and walked outside. As he phased through the front door of the opulent house, he was met by yet another strange figure.

Connecting the street to the front door of the house was a sidewalk of hard concrete that had lost most of its daytime heat. About midway between the street and the house stood a figure of black. It was dark outside save the light of the moon and the evenly spaced streetlights of the neighborhood boulevard. The shape of a man painted a stark contrast to the night scene.

The observer froze where he stood as soon as he spotted the silhouette. A momentary chill ran the length of his body as he tried to decide how to respond. A moment of indecision allowed him to inspect the man from a distance.

Outlined in moonlight, The Observer could see that he was wearing a body-length black cloak that ran from the ground, wrapped completely around him, and was tipped by a hood that covered the man's head. Had he not just had an audible conversation with the woman, he would have assumed that this figure was simply a human and posed no threat. However, he now knew that there were others here that he could interact with, and he was determined to be cautious. He placed his hand on his head and took a deep breath in preparation for a jump.

"Wait!" A husky powerful voice called out from the direction of the dark figure. "I just want to talk." The figure did not step toward him which seemed to mean for the moment he did not mean him any harm.

"Who are you?" The observer proclaimed, trying to match the authority and depth he heard in the other's voice.

"My name, spoken aloud, would bring enemies whose power rivals that of the burning sun." He paused long enough to allow for a dramatic effect. "We have not met, and I would never try to deceive you into thinking that we had." The Observer's mind raced as the implications of this statement struck him blindly.

"Are you talking about the woman who was here a moment ago?" A moment's pause came between them.

The dark one asked, "Have you been visited? I wonder if you could show me by whom?" Without hesitation, The Observer pulled from his coat pocket his leather book and pencil. Flipping to a fresh page, he illustrated a perfect image of the woman he had been conversing with moments ago. He then held it up for the dark man to see. The voice from the cloak came with a deliberate tone. "Her name is Ruth. I've seen her in the comings and goings of this place. What did she want?"

"She seemed to know me and wanted me to go with her." He waited for a response.

"I do not intend to be insulting to you, my friend, but it seems to me that you are young in the ways of interaction. If you were as free with your information in your visit with her as you are with myself, you could have very easily compromised your safety. Please tell me you did not acquiesce without proof of her claim to familiarity."

A rush of pride came over The Observer as he explained, "I gave up no information. I required from her a show of good faith that she could not produce but could only make promise of." There was again a long moment of silence as the two parties looked at each other.

Finally, the deep voice came from the cloak. "Would you be willing to share your name with me, friend?"

"In all of my recorded memory, I have never had either knowledge of or need for a name. As far as I am aware, I have none." At this, the cloaked man stepped forward ever so slightly.

"My friend, all creatures, whether terrestrial or celestial, have a name." He let this soak in for a moment before he spoke again. "It seems to me that if she truly knew you, she would be able to speak your given name. I think you did right by refusing her company."

The observer was washed with contradicting emotions at this statement. If this figure was right, he had a name. He longed to know whether this was true. He felt that the most profitable reaction would be one that did not reveal his eagerness to know his given name.

"I did not say I refused her company. I would have been satisfied to remain in her company indefinitely. I simply could not acquiesce to her request until she bore proof of the nature of her familiarity. I will request that you not twist my words. I choose them carefully and do not mean a thing by them that I do not say. As for all creatures possessing a name, I know nothing of that."

The sound of clapping broke the silence after his stern statement. The dark cloaked man clapped his hands together three times loudly. The observer had seen the humans do this when they approved of a performance.

"Bravo, my friend. You have an authority that is refreshing and quite rare." His clapping allowed the Observer to see the hands of the dark man revealed in the night light. He thought he could make out a strange texture on the surface of his skin. The limited light kept him from full visual disclosure. The cloak spoke again. "Your name is Truss."

The observer breathed deeply, noting the boldness of the statement. His mind jumped, trying to absorb such an important piece of information. He tried his best to stay calm as he replied, "How do you know this?"

"I was told by another. He has sent for you by name. He requested you come to him." At this, the dark figure unhooded his head. The evening's moon glow was enough to reveal that his skin was covered in numerous scars. Marks that were stroked in every direction wrapped all the way around his bald head. Below the scar tissue, his face was chiseled and strong. He seemed as if he had fought his way through a thousand battles, or possibly been tortured horribly. "Do not be startled by my appearance." He paused before adding, "I was told to only request your presence."

The Observer studied what he had just heard. Is it possible? Could my name actually be Truss? It seemed a fine name. He was amazed at how quickly his world was changing now.

"And what if I choose not to come?" He asked after a few long moments of contemplation.

"I am to let you leave and not hinder you thence." He paused to let the implications of the statement sink in. "However, he made it clear that I was to tell you that he can provide you with the answers that you seek, answers that you will not be able to find anywhere else."

The observer thought about the offer of answers. It was almost intoxicating to imagine finding out anything about himself. He replied authoritatively, "I will need to see some proof of good faith."

"He anticipated that you would. He is aware of your visions." The dark figure stepped forward again. His eyes were deep and intense. "He told me that you have been having visions. Visions about a unique world."

The observer was cut to the heart. He could not imagine how anyone of any station would have any more trustworthy information. This person sent for him by name and knew his thoughts. In his mind's eye, he saw the green planet, the blinding star, and the immense mountain range he had seen in his vision.

"You may call me Truss." He said with a smile. His elation rose in his chest. His excitement was palpable, and his heart began to beat fast. Finally, after a century of isolation, he would have answers. He at once began to let his mind dig up all the questions he had been saving. Although he was excited, he kept his exterior composed and calm. He stepped forward in anticipation of joining the cloaked figure.

As he did, the cloaked man did the same. They slowed as they closed the distance between themselves. He now looked upon the man's face with studied intensity. There were scars upon scars buried deep into the flesh of his powerful features. Realizing that his appearance was striking, the man spoke into the silence.

"We have long since been locked in a battle, and the evil ones have made us pay dearly for our resistance. You can understand my caution in not speaking my name aloud, but if you wish to look upon it, it is carved here."

The man pulled his cloak sleeve upward from where it rested at his wrist. With every centimeter exposed, more scars were revealed. He drew his sleeve to his elbow, which revealed that gouged deep into his forearm were ancient letters. The letters themselves must have been older than the scars because even the name itself was stacked with scar upon scar. The name, although hard to decipher, could be made out to read, "Stathos."

Truss shivered with chills as he looked at the tremendously marked surface of the man's skin. Stathos pulled his sleeve back to his wrist and reached out his hand. Truss looked at the outstretched hand, knowing that this could mean that he, too, would one day wear scars like these. With a tingle of fear, he reached out and put his hand in Stathos's.

"I will take us there," Stathos said calmly. With a flash of light, they were gone.

EXIT

THE REPEATED SOUND OF fleshy slaps echoed in the otherwise quiet hallway of Shady Oak Mental Hospital. The tile was cold and hard beneath James and Riley's feet. Riley was careful not to allow the trash bag containing their belongings, which he draped over his shoulder, to make any noise.

The time for their big escape had come. James didn't have much of a plan to draw on as they moved down the darkened corridor of the facility. He only knew that his life was going to change that night. Since they were not in a heavily secured area of the hospital, he was certain they could manage a clean getaway.

He wasn't sure how much Riley understood, but he felt confident that he hadn't brought him along against his will. Riley had been adamant when he said, "I'll be watchin' the bag, and me and dis bag will be following yo plump rump."

Both men's hearts beat rapidly, but it was hard to tell if that was due to the excitement of their current adventure or the rapid power walking they were doing down the abandoned hallway. James' blubbery girth bounced in a full-bodied jiggle underneath his hospital-issue cotton outfit. Riley was in a rare state of silence as he followed closely behind his confidant.

James held a trembling hand in the air as he slowed and then stopped at a hallway corner. The corridor ended in a perpendicular crosswalk that allowed for travel in either direction. James knew the turn well and peeked his head around the corner. He continued to hold his hand in the air, signaling Riley to halt behind. Riley had seen that gesture before, but had a totally different understanding of its meaning. Riley lifted his own hand in a similar fashion and gave James a resounding, solid high five.

Still scoping out the crosswalk, the impactful palm slap came as a total surprise. He jumped with a start, and the momentary rush of adrenaline hit his system like a freight train. His heart was really beating now, and he could feel it all the way up to his ears. He turned to Riley silently, gave a stern look, and shook his head. Riley rarely ever felt truly scorned and showed with a furrowed brow and a shrug of the shoulders that he had done nothing wrong.

James determined that the coast was clear, so he stepped out and took a hard right as he followed the wall closely. Door after door passed on both sides of the corridor as they gracelessly galloped their way to their escape.

On the left side of the hall was a small alcove that housed two vending machines. Their cool glow illuminated the passage as they approached. As the machines passed on the left, James could hear the patter of Riley's feet slowing and going off course. He looked behind to see that Riley had been drawn in by the siren call of the electronic snack vendor. Like a gravity well the alien luminosity was sucking him in. James belted out the loudest whispered rebuke he felt that he could manage in the present situation. "Riley, No! Come on! We're almost there."

Riley progressed forward as if he had heard nothing. James knew the routine and had seen it hundreds of times before. Every time they had cause to pass by the vending machines, Riley would always check the change dispenser to see if anyone had abandoned a coin. James had told him so many times how silly this practice was. Out of all the attempts Riley had pushed his old, thick-knuckled digits into the lower change slot, only twice had he pulled back a coin. Once he received a penny for his troubles, and another time he had pulled back a quarter.

These two instances had given Riley as much vindication as he would ever need. James had not foreseen this delay but now knew that it was unavoidable. Riley moved toward the machine much like a gambling addict approaches a slot machine. James half expected Riley to extend his hand and ask it to dance.

James watched as Riley poked his first two digits into the change dispenser at stomach height. To both of their surprise, the sound of a lonely coin rang out as Riley's finger raked it out into his open palm. Riley turned, looking like he had just won the million-dollar jackpot, and blurted out in a loud booming voice, "Third time's the charm!"

He held up a particularly unremarkable dime as he smiled enormously and James shushed him at top volume. James put his finger to his lips in order to remind Riley of their escape that was supposed to be silent. Riley mindfully mimicked the motion to show he remembered.

James, correctively whisper-shouted, "'Third time's the charm' means you try three times and get lucky on the third try. You tried a hundred times and only got lucky three." Riley looked inquisitively at him. James changed gears as he realized it wasn't the ideal time for a lesson in contemporaneous euphemisms. Instead, he whispered, "Come on, we're escaping, remember?"

Riley jumped back in line, and they were on the move again. As they approached the end of the hallway, there was a red glow bouncing off the walls that James knew well. They slowed and again paused at the end of the hallway where there was another turn to make. Again, James put his hand up to signal a stop was in order, but this time Riley did not slap it.

The crimson illumination of the exit sign saturated the dim waiting room at the front of the building. They were only meters from the front door and the front desk where a mostly dispassionate Brenda sat during the day. The front desk was currently empty. The glass of the front door showed the darkness of night outside.

Riley peeked around James' shoulder to see what the holdup was. They both silently stared at the doorway that represented their freedom. The red light, like so many other places, here too represented their desire. In thick letters, the sign that spelled EXIT was not an option but a command. They followed the command and made for the glass door. There was enough of the vibrant glow to navigate the sorted chairs and magazine tables that mazed the front waiting area of the hospital.

James remembered this room. This is where he sat the day that he was brought here. He had misunderstood at first what was going on. He had assumed that after the examination, he would be allowed to leave, and in actual fact, he was allowed. Dr. Thomas had talked with him as he felt a friend should: honestly and bluntly. James had enjoyed the attention he received and felt for the first time that he had been listened to. Dr. Thomas only ever encouraged him to sign himself in for an extended stay at Shady Oak for what he called "further examination and treatment."

Over the past few months... No, not months. He thought for a moment as they quietly passed through the waiting room. Had it been years? The time passed so strangely here. He had told himself many times since he checked himself in that he would leave when he wanted to, and a few times he had talked to Dr. Thomas about it. The doctor, however, was always able to talk him out of it.

James was just passive enough to be talked into signing the papers again after each three-month period was up. He had signed those papers nine times. It was this very waiting room where he had spent his last minutes as a free man. He had not so much been a prisoner of the hospital as a prisoner of his polite passivity. Well, he was doing it now. He had made the decision to leave, and that was that.

His hand rested on the bar that opened the front door. He touched it ever so lightly. His hand shook with anticipation and anxiety. He could feel Riley's hot breath swirling down the back of the neck hole on his hospital shirt. He heard his own voice come softly in a whisper, "Here we go."

It seemed to all happen at once. As soon as his hand applied pressure to the door bar, a shrieking banshee call screamed out from somewhere overhead. The deafening sound of the alarm filled his entire being with fear and another free cup of double-shot adrenaline. A fraction of a second passed before he heard a hot, loud voice ring out from behind, "Run for it, Plump-Rump!"

The crinkle of the trash bag was audible as two surprisingly sturdy hands found each of his shoulder blades and applied forward pressure. Another second and they were through the door and bolting for all they were worth, which happened to not be much. The heavy breathing began within ten steps and the quick slow down took only another fifteen.

The desire for freedom was tempered by the relative sensation of an exploding heart and fire in the lungs. The parking lot was at least twice the distance they just ran, so they stopped mid-lot for a breather. Both bent over and breathed as deeply as possible. James couldn't imagine being in more bodily distress. His lungs felt like they would dry and crack under the immense strain of breathy heaving. Riley, now wincing, grabbed at his upper leg with the hand that still held the black garbage bag.

"James?" a voice said as the alarm still screamed out from the building behind them. James turned around to see a man with bright white sneakers standing next to a shiny BMW. It was one of only a few cars left in the dimly lit parking lot at this late hour. In the evening light, Dr. Thomas' mid-scalp part was unmistakable.

They were both looking at him now as they breathed deeply. The doctor left the door of his car open and walked toward James and Riley briskly.

"What are you guys doing out here?" came the agitated voice. A day of working with the clinically insane rarely produced patient kindness. "Are you trying to escape?"

"Well... We thought we'd just go for a little jog and..." He trailed off partly because he had to take another deep breath and partly because he was not a good liar.

"'Course we escaping, butt crack part!" Riley said with a harsh inflection. He couldn't hold it, however, and gave a hearty bout of laughter.

Dr. Thomas's hand went to his head, instinctively smoothing the hairdo as he spoke loud enough to be heard over the blaring alarm. "This is ridiculous, gentlemen. Get back to your quarters at once."

"No way, no how, Butt-part," Riley said with a giggle.

The good doctor was used to being called names, but was not in the mood after this incredibly long day to stand for such insurrection.

"The alarm that you set off on your little... exodus has already alerted the police station. A patrol car will be here shortly."

"No, we don't want that," James said as he felt the heavy weight of submission beginning to squash his spirits. Still breathing heavily, he placed his hands on his knees and bent over because he thought he might throw up.

"Why would you need to escape anyway, James? You know that you can leave at any point you like, but the proper paperwork must be done first. You can't just steal out in the middle of the night. We would have thought something happened to you. It's for your own good."

"You'll never take us alive!" Riley screamed at the top of his lungs. He had regained his breath already and now began swinging the trash bag around in a circular motion above his head. "Come and get us, Dr. Butt-Part."

Dr. Thomas ignored the threat and continued looking at James as he said, "I can sign you out tomorrow morning if you want, but you have no right to lead Riley astray like this. He has to stay. You know that."

James stood upright from his squatting position and replied, "You said I had to look out for him, but I can't if I..." The doctor cut James off mid-sentence.

"That's right, you can't look out for him if you leave. We were making such good progress, I'd really hate to see you go. Not to mention how Riley would feel."

James felt that old pressure of manipulation beginning to weigh down on him as Dr. Thomas' stare bore a hole in him. Riley was still swinging the garbage bag around, and he had apparently had enough. He charged at the doctor and shouted, "To da chariot!"

With wild eyes, Riley sped toward Dr. Thomas. When he was within striking distance, he extended his range and smacked the doctor with the trash bag. Dr. Thomas crouched low, not knowing what he was being struck with. Riley kept moving quickly past and jumped into the open driver's side door of the doctor's BMW. Without closing the car door, he set the trash bag on his lap and began groping for the keys. He had the doctor's attention now.

"Riley, get out of there immediately!" Dr. Thomas bolted toward Riley and began trying to extricate him from the vehicle. The sound of police sirens swelled to commingle with the noise of the already monotonous building alarm. Riley and the doctor were grappling. James turned to see a police cruiser screaming around the corner, skidding their tires as they slid into the parking lot. James stood frozen, not knowing what to do as this avalanche of activity seemed to surround and bury him alive.

"Get yo' hands off me, you dirty ape!" Riley shouted as Dr. Thomas was trying to pull him out of the beamer.

"Riley, I've had it! Get out of my car!" He screamed back as he tried for any purchase that his hands could find. From the front seat of the car, Riley was wildly swinging like a madman.

The police car first circled near the front door of the hospital and then apparently saw the tussle happening in the doctor's car because they immediately sped over toward the action. James watched as they moved into position.

The volume of the shouting between Dr. Thomas and Riley grew to a fever pitch until the moment Riley saw the cops spring from their now parked car. In like manner, Riley sprang from the seat of the BMW and struggled free of the doctor's grasp.

"James, come on! Fall in behind me!" Riley shouted toward his stunned friend, who was simply watching the action unfold. Riley jogged with the bag in hand to the nearby edge of the parking lot and knelt down in a grassy patch between two dark trees.

As he kneeled, he thrust his hand into the garbage bag and pulled one of the cartons of milk he had been carrying, which was warm by now.

"Bombs away, pigs! I hope you like milk wit' dat bacon!" He threw the palm-sized carton of milk like a hand grenade at the two advancing police officers. The heavier of the two took a direct his in the middle of his torso. The warm milk exploded like warm blood all over the front of the policeman. It had the intended effect, and the officer slowed his pace. The other officer continued to charge for Riley.

"It does a body good, bitch!" Riley shouted as he released another volley of two airborne cartons. The first only hit near the second officer's feet, but the second was a direct hit. It splattered white creamy fluid all over his face, and it ran down into the front of his uniform.

Riley quickly fired his remaining few cartons as he shouted, but his time the cops were able to anticipate and move out of the way. When they were reasonably confident that he was out of ammunition, they charged in and tackled him hard.

"Save yo self, it's too late for me!" He shouted to James as he watched it all unfold. For an old man, Riely still had a lot of fight in him, and James thought he must have wrestled cops before because he looked pretty experienced. Just when they would almost have him in handcuffs, he would juke and fake them out. A few times, he broke free, but it looked as if the officers would quickly get the best of him. In desperation, Riley shouted again, "It's too late for me, save yourself!"

James was so deeply conflicted, and he felt that familiar feeling of rising vomit again. He had an insatiable urge to join the hopeless battle and go down with a blaze of glory, but it was the going down that had him worried. As he watched his only friend attempt to fight off a superior force, Dr. Thomas stepped into place next to him. They both watched as Dr. Thomas spoke softly now.

"They'll get him, don't worry."

James could feel the ire rise in his blood, and it was as if tremendous heat consumed his bones. He astonished himself as he realized he was about to take action. Almost without thinking, James reached back and in a wide arc he swung a wild open hand and slapped Dr. Thomas as hard as he could. He would have punched him, but was unfamiliar with the procedure and did not want to damage his fist. His aim was also bad, so instead of a square slap across the face, his hand connected with a loud clap across the side of the doctor's neck.

"I'm so sorry, Doctor, but I'm crazy as a loon," James said as Dr. Thomas recoiled from the power slap he had just received. James felt he should apologize again, but didn't want to completely undo the intense feeling of accomplishment that aggressive palm smack had just given him.

Without another word, James charged into the fray to join the greatest battle he had ever been a part of. He could hardly tell what was happening once he was in the middle of it. He momentarily thought of the depiction of fights he had seen on TV, and this was nothing like it. He couldn't be sure, but he thought later that he might have even bitten someone at some point in the midst of the dust-up.

"You slap like a girl, you little turd!" Dr. Thomas shouted as he charged into the flurry of aggression. It was a full-on free-for-all. The doctor did know how to throw a punch, and with rapid succession, he rained down blows on both Riley and James. This quickly turned the police from the enemy into allies. Riley, however, apparently didn't see the shift in group dynamics because as soon as the cops turned their attention toward the Dr., he clocked a clumsy blow on the back of the taller officer's head.

All said, the showdown lasted two minutes and thirty-six seconds, but it felt like an entire lifetime was packed into those short moments. James thought he had never felt so alive, nor had he ever felt so bruised.

In the end, it wasn't the overpowering force of the police that won the day or even their superior tactics. It was something simple that ultimately did it. It was a flash of light that no one saw except James. He turned around and set his eyes on a face that he had longed to see for a number of years now. With familiarity, he breathed the name of the figure that now stood before him.

"Ruth."

DESERT

A CHILLING GUST OF wind harassed the night sand hills of a remote desert somewhere in the world. An eruption of light and time-space pressure seized the area with a flash and dissipated as quickly as it came. The observer had fully embraced the name that this dark figure had relayed to him and had acquainted himself with it. He was now Truss.

As he took Stathos' hand Truss had imagined the green planet that he had seen in his vision. It was one of many mysteries to which he hoped to get some answers. The mountain in the dreamlike state stood ever so tall and powerful as it had in his mind.

Stathos had brought them to a desert place. Much of the night landscape was rock and sand. Truss released the hand of his new companion, and with those same hands, Stathos replaced his hood on his head.

The sky was only lit by the shimmer of a thousand distant stars. Their meager light glinted off the low-lying peaks of numerous sand dunes as far as could be seen. Arid landscapes were not unfamiliar to Truss. He had observed numerous locations much like this one, but did not recognize anything about the place he had just been brought to.

"We will have to walk from here. We have some of the best worm guards in this galaxy watching the stronghold." Stathos said with a tinge of pride.

Truss followed his footsteps as he asked, "What is a worm guard?"

Stathos stopped cold and turned to truss. He stared at him for a long moment before he spoke. "She really emptied you out, didn't she?" With the look of pity in his eyes, he laid a strong scarred hand on Truss' shoulder and said, "I'm so glad we found you when we did." Truss said nothing as he waited for a response to his question.

Stathos turned and continued to walk as he explained in a deep, friendly manner. "We just transported ourselves from one side of this planet to another. The terrestrial creatures, like the ones you've been observing, are spatially limited to linear travel. Celestials, like you or I, have the ability to manipulate time-space in such a way that we can move from one four-dimensional location to another nonlinearly." Stathos stopped walking momentarily to look back at Truss. When he saw that he had his full attention, he continued.

"This creates temporary tubular structures through time-space that allow us to traverse vast distances in no time. Since we've been trapped here so long, we've begun to borrow quite a few terms from the humans. Some of their wise men call this type of spatial tube a wormhole. A worm guard is a celestial that can sense another's wormhole. She can take a wormhole and close it off so that the traveler can't jump to where he wants. If she has some level of skill, she can take the wormhole and turn it in on itself, putting the end at the mouth of the beginning, which effectively traps the traveler. If she's very good, she can redirect it entirely or even seal it off with the traveler inside it."

Now at the crest of a sand dune, Stathos stopped and allowed Truss to step to the top with him. They looked out over the sandy desert expanse. The wind whipped them jaggedly as they stood admiring the starlit scene.

"So why are we here?" Truss asked with enthusiasm. He felt a rush of excitement as he anticipated another helping of cosmic answers. Stathos turned to him and spoke crisply.

"That's a question for the Archetype."

"The Archetype?" Truss asked with a hidden thrill.

"The Archetype is the one who summoned you. You will meet soon enough, and she can answer those types of questions much more successfully than I." With an eagerness that was hard to hide, Truss tried again.

"Why are you trapped on this planet?"

"Enough questions." Stathos barked with an intensity that startled Truss. It was clear that Stathos was not getting the same level of enjoyment from this game. Truss composed himself and quieted his eagerness. After a deep breath and a short silence, Stathos spoke curtly.

"Where we are about to go, I am not in charge. I'm only a servant. Many of my warrior brothers would love nothing more than to tear you to pieces. You are not to speak until we reach the Archetype. Even the sound of your voice could send my brothers into a rage, and I would not be able to protect you." Stathos paused and looked at him. Truss noticed an unfamiliar pull at the corner of Stathos' eyes. Was it contempt? Stathos spoke even more bitterly this time. "Take that stupid hat off."

With surprising aggression, Stathos grabbed the top hat and slung it to the ground. It rolled down the sand dune and out of sight. A swelling bubble of misgiving was beginning to grow in Truss's mind. The two figures continued step by step into the night.

By the time they reached a discernible destination, the temperature had dropped another few degrees, and the sandy wind swirled about them with an unforgiving strength. They had been following the ridge of a sand dune for quite some time, and the moon was beginning its ascent into the dry, windy night.

Without any notice, two figures in the shape of men were standing in front of Truss and Stathos. They appeared without a flash of light or a noise. The stealthy men were apparelled in dark cloaks similar to the one Truss had been made to wear. They were, however, enormous. Truss, standing at a full postured height, would not even be able to reach one of these men's shoulders with outstretched hands. He thought they must have been twice his height. Are these the warriors that Stathos had spoken of? They stood like deadly statues cloaked in black, hooded night.

Stathos stepped forward in familiarity and addressed them in muffled tones. Truss kept his distance, realizing that he felt something unfamiliar. Was it fear that was pumping in his blood? He bowed his head slightly to obscure his face as Stathos spoke with the two men in a language that he could not make out.

Although still unintelligible, the booming voice of one of the giant figures returned response to Stathos. It seemed to echo and rumble. Truss was sure now, it was fear that gripped him. This was a fresh experience. He had seen fear many times in the creatures he had observed on this world, but had never felt it himself.

Something in their conversation made them all three look at Truss. The massive heads of the two giant warriors tilted up to catch a full glimpse as Stathos turned his head to peer at him. They all turned back to their private council and continued their discussion. Truss felt the undeniable feeling of terror as he imagined those enormous juggernauts tearing him piece by piece.

The experience was all new to him. He had never in all his recorded memory imagined his own demise and it surprised him how vividly it came. He attempted to maintain a sense of composure as the conversation that would determine his fate continued. The moon was high in the sky before their conversation had finished. Stathos turned and stepped toward Truss as he spoke.

"They offer you passage. Do not speak or stray from the path that they set out."

Without warning, the two giants were beside him. There was no flash of light and no path in the sand. One of the enormous warriors laid his hand on Truss's upper back and wrapped his first finger and thumb around the entirety of his neck and throat. The heat of fear rose in pitch, echoing around in his mind. The great celestial soldier, however, did not apply excess pressure. The finger and thumb formed an iron-clad shackle about his neck that he would not be able to escape. A second later, the other Juggernaut spoke to Stathos with a thundering boom.

"Lead on."

Stathos led the dark procession of celestial beings. Behind him, Truss stepped carefully forward between two enormous war giants. He tried to calm the inner images of his own destruction. He reminded himself that this warrior's shackled grasp was simply a precaution, and they did not intend to destroy him. Although he tried, he was not able to completely subjugate the intense fear that was shooting like a volcano into his consciousness. Some ancient awareness seemed to be screaming to him, "Don't go with these creatures!" They all knew, however, that no matter what his level of anxiety was, there was now no way to escape. He had willingly stuck his neck out and was now quite certain it was a trap.

Within the next few steps Stathos took a hard right and began to descend down the steep sand dune. Truss and his two guards followed him down. When they reached the bottom of the sand dune Truss was surprised to find that they continued their descent even after the landscape had evened out around them.

It was as if there were hidden stairs beneath the terrain, and with each step, the sand around the foursome fanned and cleared out of their way. As they progressed downward into and below the surface, it was as if a bubble of empty space surrounded them. The bubble pushed the earth out of the way in a spherical shape as they moved toward its edge. Within a few steps, they had bored below the horizon point.

Truss began to notice the sound around them. As they continued down, the bubble of open space closed in with sand behind them. The noise of sandy crackle and gritty friction grew to a heavy rumble. Truss had been in some very extreme subterranean depths before, but he had never seen such a trick.

They walked as if a slanted surface lay beneath them but he noticed that it was simply a bed of sand no different than the dune he had walked down moments before. The bubble of free space followed them down as it repelled the sand before them and closed in behind.

As they magically burrowed into the earth, Truss noticed a faint orange glow emanating from the surface of the sand bubble that was constantly forming and reforming around them. After watching closely with rapt curiosity, he discovered that the orange glow was created by millions of swirling grains of sand that were reaching the silica molten point due to the immense friction that they were being subjected to. The crackling sound then must be that of cooling and hardening glass cracking as the same force of friction shatters the newly formed microstructures. He wished he could pull his book out and make a few notes and take down a drawing or two, but he decided against it when he remembered the shackled fingers encircling his throat. His fear converted at least some of its own mass into wonder as he imagined the great power of these dark creatures that escorted him to the depths.

They walked into the sandy reaches of the planet for what seemed like decades until they reached an underground rock formation. As the sand and earth cleared out in front of them, a great cavernous stone mouth stood open like a gaping entrance to a subterranean world. Truss noticed the rigid recoil of his footfall as they passed under and through the craggy entrance of the cavern mouth. The sand bubble closed behind them and stood as a disciplined wall of earth that would progress no further than the mouth of the underground cave.

More enormous cloaked figures stood guard in the dark crevices of the rock tunnel. He counted sixteen mountainous creatures like the two that escorted him down, standing at the ready near the cave opening. As Stathos approached, the massive juggernauts stepped aside to allow them passage. The giant cave guards watched as they passed. Truss had never thought he would become so familiar with the sensation of paralyzing fear, but it seemed with every step, a new terror was waiting in the dark.

Step by step they plodded deeper into the subterranean stronghold. At every turn of the rock tunnel there were massive war giants and each seemed larger than the last. At unpredictable intervals the way would, from time to time, open up into a cavern room; Some of them small and some of them impossibly large. In the larger of these rooms the cave walls would fan out and diverge to create a massive gathering space.

The first of the large gathering spaces that they came to allowed Truss yet another unexpected experience. The narrow passageway of rock channeled toward them the echoing murmur of what sounded like a crowd of voices. The chatter could have been mistaken for a busy marketplace of any large city in the human world, mixed with the natural acoustic reverb that the cave walls provided. He knew that they must be approaching an open place in the cave formation because the sound was growing louder.

When they finally stepped through the opening to the huge rock chamber the sound changed immediately. What was idle chatter grew to only intermittent whisper in a fraction of a second. As Truss adjusted his eyes for the massive distances that stood before him in the chamber he realized that he had just stepped into a room with thousands of spectators. There was a clear cut path through the center of the voluminous cave space.

At each side of the path and up the walls the surface of the rock slanted jaggedly. At different spaces along the rigid surface there were varying juts and crevices. At each place where there was a break in the surface of the rock there were gathered pockets of creatures who were now staring at the four figured crew that passed through on the cave chamber floor.

Thousands of sets of eyes watched with deep interest at the captive that was being escorted through the dark depths. The creatures that Truss could see well enough to identify had mostly the common shape of men and women. Some were large like his captors, and some were smaller than himself. The horde to which the thousands of staring eyes belonged was not cloaked, however. They stood naked and white skinned in the dim shadows of the rock.

When they had passed about three-quarters of the way through the chamber, Truss got a good look at a group who were hiding in a shallow, craggy recess about ten paces from the path. Without dark cloaks, he could see that they were pale and lean. Like Stathos, their skin was marked by scars, and not a square centimeter on any of them was free of wounded markings. Their beady, greedy eyes seemed to bore into him.

Without any warning, shouts erupted and echoed off the stone walls of the chamber. It started behind them but enveloped the room like a wave. Within seconds, the entire gathering space was full of pale scarred figures shouting, screeching, and howling like ravenous animals. Truss could see the small band in the nearby crag had joined in. Their darkened yellow teeth stood like broken mountains in their dry, cracked gums as they shouted unintelligibly at him. Was that even possible? They were shouting at him? Some jumped up and down, some slapped the rock, but all screamed like jackals. Aggression poured from their mouths as the angry tumult coalesced into a cacophony of agitated yelps.

Truss felt his heart now racing at full throttle. He looked up at the war giant that still had two iron fingers around his neck. He hoped to find some solace in the face of the juggernaut. Realizing he was being looked at, the captor glanced down at Truss and gave a slight grin. In his deep, powerful voice, he spoke loud enough to be heard over the battery of echoing screeches.

"Welcome to Molgathra." The other juggernaut laughed loudly at his companion's wry jest. The shouting climaxed into a thunder of screeching before the pathway narrowed back down into a corridor. As they walked on, he felt relieved to be out of the cavern chamber.

As they moved through the enormous system of caves, Truss made a mental map of every step. Many times he felt the urge to make drawings in his book of the fascinating underground world he was touring, but made no move for his sketch book.

After another extended time of walking, they came to a place where the corridor opened up to about four times a man's height. As they moved through this widened pass, Truss noticed what he thought to be carved cells in the rock walls on either side of the cave. The cells were occupied, but the creatures within were not the scarred, pale men he had seen in the gathered darkness of the previous vast chamber. These figures were large like his escorts, but had skin that was smooth and clean.

Those in the rock cells were not clothed but stood with all of their appendages in full extension. As he passed the first cell, Truss saw that their hands, feet, and head were all buried in the solid rock walls of the cells that they occupied. Are these prisoners? He dared not ask aloud. He reasoned that they might be imprisoned warriors who were taken in battle.

The parts of the bodies that were not obscured by the rock formation of the cells seemed powerful and dangerous. Their tight skin looked like polished bronze and was stretched over bulging musculature. As they continued to walk, they passed hundreds of stone prisons that were all occupied. Some struggled against the rock.

"Impressive, isn't it? I told you the enemy had taken so much from us, I didn't tell you of the prisoners we have taken of theirs." Stathos said without turning to look in Truss' direction. They continued on as he looked intently at the imprisoned figures. "It's not actually the rock that holds them. It's the power of the Archetype."

When they had passed through twelve large chambers, nine small gathering places, been seen by thousands upon thousands of pale screeching creatures, and taken six thousand four hundred and nineteen steps they came to a massive doorway made of stone.

Although it could be called a door, the structure that stood before them more closely resembled a tombstone of astronomical size. It was not masterfully carved but instead beaten and chipped out of one solid piece of rock. The stone door did not serve the purpose of a decorative first impression. It seemed to have been created without any thought of aesthetics at all.

Stathos stopped in front of the giant stone that blocked the passage, and Truss's two guards forced him to pause behind him. Now that they stood still, Truss took in the entire scene. The corridor, which had been narrow, opened up into a greater height as it approached the place where the stone door sat. The path that they were on was worn smooth underfoot and led from the previously narrow cave, which progressed directly underneath where the large rock door sat.

A grinding rumble began to be audible from the direction of the stone doorway. The sound quickly grew to an immersive noise echoing off the hard walls around them. The stone, as large as it stood, was moving. A centimeter at a time, it groaned against the rigid floor of the cave as it slid slowly open.

The darkness of the portion of cave they were in was contrasted by an orange glowing shaft of light that broke through and cast itself in a vivid beam on the floor and walls. More light spilled through as the door opened. When a body width had been opened between the cave wall and the stone door, Truss could see an enormous uncloaked juggernaut silhouetted by the light. His meaty, man-sized hands braced squarely against the door and were heaving it out of the way. The massive brute glanced toward Stathos and then Truss. When he realized how small the visitors were, he stopped shoving. The sound died, and the door became immediately still.

The silhouetted brute disappeared behind the still half-closed door, and the full flow of the light poured through the opening. Stathos, who had been facing the door, turned toward the juggernaut who was still holding Truss' neck in an iron-fingered shackle. He gestured to him, and Truss immediately felt that the hold had been released. He looked over to the place where the war giant had stood, but he wasn't there. He then looked over to where the other hulking giant had just been, and he too was gone.

The glint of orange light bounced from Stathos' un-hooded head.

"The Archetype's chamber," Stathos said as he presen-tationally extended his hand toward the illuminated open-ing. Truss glanced at him briefly and then stepped forward toward the open door.

Truss squinted as he stepped through the aperture in the rock doorway. The chamber was small and lit by firelight. Strangely, it did not have the look of a subterranean dun-geon, as did most of the passageways leading to this point. There were the familiar rigid walls of rock, but on the surface of each wall was hung patterned fabric decoration.

The firelight came from a candle perched on a rock ledge carved into the far wall of the room.

Truss stepped cautiously into the room and looked around. The huge hulk that had serviced the stone doorway was now standing to the right of the opening. He towered above Truss as his large, dark eyes followed the guest's meek footsteps. The brute was much like the others, but up close, Truss could see that this creature was not covered in scars. He had some markings, no doubt from battles long past, but his wounds must not have been as severe because there were only intermittent patches of scar tissue scattered around his enormous frame.

His thick, muscular build seemed to be packed beneath mostly smooth skin of brushed steel. Even his head was packed with girth upon muscle. Truss tried his best not to cower in front of the massive personage. He stepped in front of the big creature, looked him in the eye, and waited.

This must be the Archetype, Truss thought. Stathos, who was apparently waiting outside had told him not to speak and he intended to follow his instructions. The brute, seemed confused as he tilted his head slightly and returned Truss' stare. A voice that was frail, weathered, and unexpected broke the silence.

"What do you want with my doorman?"

The voice was cracked and dry. Truss turned in the direction it came from and saw, sitting in a small chair near the candle, an old, bent woman. As soon as they locked eyes, He knew that this was the Archetype. His subconscious led him to step away from the dangerous doorman and toward the middle of the small room.

Her deep-set eyes were storm-cloud grey, surrounded by pale skin that was as dry as desert sand. The wrinkles that spiraled out from her eyes spoke of her incredible age. She stayed seated in a frail and feeble position. She wore the knitted clothes of a human grandmother, but didn't have that familiar sweet old lady demeanor behind her stare. "I thought you were going to vaporize my doorman, and I'm sure you can imagine how hard it is to find good help."

Truss turned and glanced back at the enormous brute who was still staring at him. Truss, however, still did not speak. After another long moment, the Archetype continued. "That's right, Truss, they are scared of you. It's been a long time since someone quite like you has been to this world." She watched him for a response, but he was still uncertain whether he should speak. She shifted in her chair as if even sitting there was uncomfortable. She reached up too slowly and used a long, bony finger to scratch her stringy white hair. Her entire scalp moved slightly as she dug her nail into and then raked across her scalp.

"Doorman," she croaked, "leave us, I'm afraid this warrior is finding it difficult not to attack and devour you."

Truss heard the shuffling of giant feet across the rock floor as the hulking doorman stepped out of the room. Truss could feel himself calm a little. The aged woman tried again. "It's difficult when you're abandoned, I know the feeling."

Truss' eyes widened slightly and he felt a rush of excitement as he began to relax enough to remember why he came. He still was cautious not to speak. This time with more compassion in her voice she almost sang. "Have you been so removed from yourself that you cannot speak?"

He nervously took a breath and drank in his fear as his words came out. "Why have you summoned me here?"

"Ahh, you are able." She smiled a little crooked but pleasant smile as she adjusted herself again. "I thought we might be able to help you."

"How could you help me?"

"You are looking for answers. I already know some of your questions, and I can show you how to find the answers to others."

This filled him with hope. He could hardly soak in the gravity of such a situation. For over a century, he had deeply wished for this moment, and now it was upon him. With enthusiasm, he began.

"Who am I?"

"We've watched you for a little over a century now but only recently been able to communicate with you. What we know is that you are from another world but because of our limited communication and resources we don't know which of the worlds you come from."

Truss let this sink in for a long moment, allowing the comfort of a few breaths to wash over him before he made eye contact again. When he did, he tried another angle. "Is there a way to find out who I am?"

"You would not have traveled here alone. Your people would have considered that too dangerous for various reasons. In cases like yours, your memories would be removed and entrusted to a partner that guards and protects both you and your memories. In the normal course of time, when your task is done, your memories should be returned to you, but we believe something went wrong."

Her words seemed to echo off the hard walls of the room. He tried to ingest the information as quickly as possible in order to receive another helping, but his mind was racing at light speed. A thought slammed into him like a train car.

"The woman who appeared to me?" He trailed off.

"Her name is Ruth, and we have reason to believe that she has been trying to sabotage you and your work here."

She stopped for a long moment, coughed loudly, and then spit on the ground. Truss fired back quickly.

"What has she done?"

"She has placed your memories in a vessel where they don't belong. She will claim to be unable to return them to you."

Truss deflated as he envisioned the woman with the pretty, round face. With less enthusiasm, he continued, "So I will never know who I am and what I'm supposed to do?"

"I did not say that. I said that she would retrieve them. What she cannot do, I can. Bring the vessel to me and I will do what she cannot. I will give you the answers that you are looking for." Truss brightened mildly, realizing that there was still hope.

"Why would you do this for me?"

"I plan to help you because I want your help in return."

Truss shifted where he stood, realizing that he had just made a terrible assumption. Why would he have thought he was getting something for nothing? He braced himself for what would come next. The ancient woman's cracking voice came again.

"It's nothing difficult or compromising, I simply need a one-time transportation. My people here are not able to do it for various reasons, and I need an outsider like yourself to do it." Truss realized he must have contorted his face in confusion because she waved a knuckled hand through the air as if to reassure him. He squinted as he asked his next question.

"Will you be expecting me to join your..." he paused to search for the right word, "Your... group?" The old woman laughed vigorously.

"No! By no means. It is, in fact, imperative that you do not join the ranks of Molgathra. The mission I have for you would not work if you did." She reached up and scratched her ear before she continued.

"Early in our struggle, we battled across the entire solar system, but in the last few millennia, our enemy has found a way to bind us to this planet. They have worm guards that trap any of the Molgathra who try to travel away. I have grown old and long to finish my days somewhere other than this stinking cave. If I can gain passage from one who is not of Molgathra, we will pass unnoticed and I can find a restful place to die in peace."

Truss felt obliged to give words to her obvious pain, but had none to share. He simply stood and watched her. He imagined getting his memories back. The thought grew until it was so immense that it filled his entire mind. He finally spoke.

"I can do this for you and will do my best to make it happen." She stood immediately and clapped her pasty hands together. Her face showed an enormous, crooked smile. She stepped toward him and spoke in a whispered tone.

"It is important that you do not speak of this meeting with Ruth, we do not yet know where she stands." He nodded but felt it was wrong to make any promises until he waited to see Ruth's so called show of good faith. He realized that his meeting was coming to an end but he still had numerous questions.

"What about my vision?"

"It will all be cleared up when you return, but I can't go into it now for various reasons." Her voice cracked at the end of the statement, and with that, the meeting was over. She thanked him, sat back down, and Stathos came in to usher him out. But what about my visions? He kept the words to himself but felt more than a little cheated.

THE VISITING

THE RAIN SEEMED TO splash down in huge gulps. It splattered along the muddy edge of an old abandoned gas station as it fell from the leaky roof edge. The glow of a single street light danced vibrantly in the reflection as a million droplets smashed into the earth.

The gas station had sat vacant for years now, and no one seemed to know why it hadn't been pulled down by this point. The paint had peeled off of the two pumps that were probably installed somewhere in the mid-1950s.

The surrounding farmland had continued to modernize while this station was left for the powerful arm of time to ravage. The dirt road gushed its orange blood of muddy waves into the ditches at either side.

A pop and flash of greenish blue light flared off the station wall and pump, and then dissipated as quickly as it came. In the rain, now stood three people who were quickly getting soaked. James and Riley, who were quite used to the rain but not inner-dimensional time-space travel, both put their hands to their stomachs. Ruth, who was used to inner-dimensional travel but was quite unused to being pelted by rain, put her hands to her face. After she inspected the wetness, she spoke.

"It feels so weird to be materialized. It feels like I'm being bombarded by..." She trailed off before she finished the sentence. A smile crept across Riley's face.

"Ya gettin' hit by raindrops 'da size of watermelons!" Riley blurted. They all looked around for some shelter. The old pump station cover was still standing, so they moved toward it and out of the rain. Once they found a spot that wasn't too leaky, Ruth inspected her hands and touched her face again.

"It still feels strange, I haven't fully materialized in a long time." James was watching her intently by now. His eyes traced the curves of her face. It took him a long moment before he had the courage to speak.

"I thought you were just a vision. I'd just about convinced myself I was nuts." A long pause, and only the sound of the rain stood between them. James moved toward Ruth with an awkward double baby step and reached out his hand. He had Ruth's full attention now and slowed as he approached. He grazed the backside of his hand across her cheek, and as the knuckles touched her wet skin, she pulled a startled breath.

"She real?" Riley asked still a little too loudly.

"She's real."

"Good cause I'z startin to think I might had caught whatever kind a crazy you got." Riley chuckled and mumbled a little to himself, but the other two stood locked into a strange kind of uneasy stare. James put his hand down as Ruth wiped the wetness from her face with the back of her hand. A moment of indecision passed between them before anything happened. James was the first to snap out of it.

"This is the woman I told you about," James said as he turned to Riley. He pointed his finger at her face as he continued. "She came to me like I told you, remember? She is a…" James trailed off as he thought for a short second. "Uh, well, what are you exactly?" She took a breath to speak, but Riley blurted before she was able.

"She's an alien, I seen her type before.. look all cute right before she probe yo plump rump." This time Riley didn't laugh but just looked at her harshly. Now James spoke up again.

"Remember how I told you I could teleport? It's just like I said." James' excitement was higher each time. "Have you come to take us off-world?" Without a beat, Riley added in.

"Or to probe our butts?" They both stared at her and waited for her response. Her enormous eyes hid behind her glasses as she wished she had not just broken one of the most important galactic directives. What could she do? She had to repair the broken situation she had created. She glanced at them both before she spoke.

"It just feels so strange." She turned, walked away, and stood at the edge of the rainfall as James and Riley looked at each other, baffled. James stepped forward and joined her. They watched the rain as it came down from the hidden sky. The glint of the street light shone off every drop that passed.

They could hear Riley mumbling something behind them as he made some noise. It sounded like he was rummaging through the old remains of the broken-down station. They paid no attention to him as they watched the rain. Ruth thought of her next step, and James thought of her.

"Time ta die space witch!" Riley screamed at the top of his lungs. As the words hurled from his spit-splattering mouth, he ran at his top speed toward Ruth. In his hands was the only weapon he could find in the busted rubble of the station. Above his head, he wielded a thick, rusted iron pipe. Before James could react, Riley swung with all his strength and smashed Ruth across the back of the head with the enormous metal weapon.

The pipe came down hard and made a solid thud as it crashed the crown of Ruth's head. The expected did not follow, however. Rather than fall to the ground writhing in bloody pain, Ruth turned around slowly. By the time she turned, Riley had dropped the pipe and was holding his right wrist as if the impact had hurt him. He looked up slowly, knowing now that she was possibly dangerous.

"I'm so sorry." She said gently, "Have I hurt you?" She calmly reached out and touched his wrist. Riley recoiled at the touch and stepped backwards, determined to keep his distance.

Ruth turned around to make sure James was not hurt as well. He was holding and inspecting the iron pipe closely. He squinted in a harsh stare of amazement as he turned the pipe over and over.

"It's cast Iron!" He said with full astonishment.

"Perfect for probing butts!" Riley said with scorn in his voice. James looked from the pipe to Ruth as he spoke.

"So, what are you?" A deep breath and long pause made her response seem more dramatic than she intended it to be.

"I'm not like you, strictly speaking, and I never intended to involve you in all this mess." She paused to gather her thoughts before she spoke again. "I'm here on behalf of my friend, and I need your help."

"Don't let her get behind you!" Riley shouted coldly.

She looked in Riley's direction kindly. "I'm not here to hurt either of you." She attempted a smile that was little more than strange and didn't wear it well, as if her face was more used to expressions that came along with worry. Turning to James, she asked, "Do you remember when I appeared to you?"

"How could I forget it? Kind of a defining moment." He smiled proudly, recalling the feeling of that experience. "Knowing my true identity changed my life. It was like my eyes were suddenly open." He looked at her intently, hoping for some clarity or explanation. Her words came slow and were riddled with uncertainty.

"I did something terrible that day, I gave you something that I had no right to give. Before I knew it... It was done, and I couldn't do anything about it without hurting you." Her eyes sank to the ground as if she had just confessed something horrendous.

James had no idea what she meant by the riddle. He turned it over in his mind, but nothing made sense. He scrunched his face up in confusion as he replied. "Well, just tell me what it is. I'll return it."

"That's the problem. You can't." Tears began to well up around the edges of her eyes. Riley and James looked at each other once again, baffled. Riley shrugged his shoulders and took a seat, leaning his back against the old gas pump. The rain softened, and the sound of a truck splashing in the distance filled the empty moment. It was James who broke the silence.

"I don't know what to do, but I'm sure I can help if you'll explain what you mean." Now, a full tear ran down Ruth's face. She sobbed lightly and wiped her cheek with the back of her hand. She took another deep breath and began to explain.

"After I touched you that day, you suddenly felt like you had new memories, right?" James nodded and waited with bated breath as he knew a long-awaited explanation was on its way. She continued. "I gave you someone else's memories. I was supposed to be guarding them until he needed them again." She took a moment to catch her breath. "I saw you there and knew that you were in distress. I knew that if you could see some of the things that I've seen, you would understand that there is so much more beyond this." She stopped to gauge how he was taking it. James looked down at the ground, processing what he had just heard.

"So I'm not Truss?" He finally said after a long moment of contemplation.

"No, I'm so sorry." The utter pain of the moment washed over her as she tried to stay in control of her emotions. "I just wanted to show you a glimpse of life outside this world. I didn't know how to stop the flow without tearing all of your memories away. Your brain is not like ours; it's soft and pliable, and I would have ripped it to pieces if I tried." She paused. "I could have stopped it, but it would have killed you."

James sat very still while he took all of it in. With an, I knew it was too good to be true tone of voice he finally broke the silence.

"I guess it never quite made sense why I'd be cosmically important," James said as he visibly deflated. He sulkily slumped and plodded over to the rubble where the broken gas pumps stood. Riley made space for him as he turned and sat on the edge of the concrete pad. She watched him and then stepped toward them slowly. She was reminded of the night she first saw him.

"You were so sad, I knew you were going to hurt yourself. I'm not supposed to be involved in terrestrial affairs

on this planet, but I couldn't stand to see you commit..."
She stopped short.

"Suicide?" James finished her sentence. He closed his
eyes as he remembered that night. "I was so excited that
I had some purpose." He opened his eyes, "I thought I
was cosmically important." He laughed ironically. Ruth
chimed in energetically.

"But James, you are!" He looked up at her as she continued. "Maybe not in the way you thought, but now,
because of my mistake, you are important." She thought
for a second. "Very important, actually. I hadn't seen it that
way, but actually, you have an incredibly vital role to play
in a cosmological drama." She knew she was beginning to
hit a chord as she watched James light up a little. His mood
began to brighten.

"She got her tracker beam focused on yo' plump rump."
Riley blurted. They both had almost forgotten he was
there. They glanced at him momentarily. He had silently
scooted halfway, hiding behind the remains of the second
gas pump on the far side of the concrete pad when she
approached. His dark, fearful eyes scanned them madly.
They both turned back to the conversation at hand.

"James, I am very sorry for what I did to you, but I
absolutely need your help." She was standing over him
now, and she knew she had him. She could see it in his

eyes. She reached out her hand and offered it to him. He grabbed it lightly and let her strength pull him to his feet. Now, face to face, they stood in close proximity.

James could feel the electricity of the moment. He could tell that this was a powerful second in time. He leaned toward her ever so slightly, closed his eyes, and puckered his eager lips.

"What are you doing?" Ruth asked with true curiosity.

"Go for it!" Riley shouted with a level of fervor that was as heartfelt as his attempted murder with the pipe. Apparently, his desire to behold carnal intimacy was indistinguishable from his drive to commit homicide.

James opened his eyes with a flush of intense embarrassment. He knew from past experience that he was notoriously bad at reading the intentions of the female gender. Once, as a young boy, he had tried to hold a girl's hand on the playground because he had noticed her looking at him. She jerked her hand away, and to add insult to injury, he realized why she had been staring. He had a tail of toilet paper hanging from the back of his pants. Not much had changed since the fourth-grade playground.

He knew that he had misread the situation. She had not offered him her hand because she was inviting a kiss from her hero. She had simply meant what she said. She needed his help. He made a mental note not to assume that a woman ever means anything other than what she says.

"Uh, well, in this world, when two people make an agreement, they kiss." He said with a tinge of guilt, knowing that it was mostly a lie. He could only think of one type of agreement that began with a kiss, and he was now certain that casual sex was not what this beautiful alien woman was after. "Never mind, I'd be glad to help you."

"Wonderful! So here's what we need to..." She stopped herself in mid-sentence and spun around so fast that she was almost invisible for a split second. James moved around to get a better look at her face. She was visibly disturbed.

"What's wrong?" He asked with true concern in his voice.

"They've found us." She whispered with an obvious tone of fear soaking through her words. "Coming this way, three bound ones... Molgathrians!" Standing where she was, she turned her face toward James and whispered, "Wait for me here." She suddenly disappeared. There was no flash of light or sound; she simply vanished.

ESCORT

STATHOS AND THE TWO juggernauts escorted Truss back out of the caverns of Molgathra, up through the sand, and back to the peak of the sand dune that they had been on before descending into the caves.

"You can jump from here." Stathos said after stopping suddenly. Truss realized that the enormous hand that had been around his neck on the journey in and out of the buried stronghold was now gone. He looked to the right and left and both of the war giants were nowhere to be seen. That was a cool trick, he wished he knew how to do it.

Free of his guards, Truss observed his surroundings. It was the same desert sand on which they had previously stood. The night air was cooler than when they had burrowed into the ground. The moon was not out, but the light glint of starlight rimmed Stathos's silhouette.

Stathos now stood facing Truss. He spoke again. "The Archetype has paid you an incredible honor by choosing you to assist in her plan." Finally being free of the caves, Truss felt the urge to speak freely.

"What about my vision? She didn't offer any answers." Truss said as he watched Stathos' face intently. He thought he saw a wave of frustration move across Stathos' face, but then subside. He had the sense that this interaction was taking incredible self-control on the part of this dark-cloaked stranger.

"The Archetype is wise and her ways are sound," Stathos said with an air of uninterested avoidance.

Stathos did not seem to be very keen on offering up information, and this was altogether strange to Truss. He felt the puzzle pieces spinning and trying to fit together in his mind. Why would anyone need to avoid questions unless they were hiding something? The thought almost seemed like a light in the distance of his mind. Was it possible that these creatures were not what they seemed to be?

"Why do you not answer questions directly?" Truss said without a pause. This direct approach caught Stathos harshly as if he had taken a blow across the chin. His eyes deepened with dark brooding for a short second but as if he was choking down the taste of bile he slowed his breath and regained control.

Truss thought of the myriad mysteries of this strange personage. He seemed to be so intensely volatile. What type of environment could produce such an alien strain of entities? The Archetype had talked of wars. Truss thought that this must be the root of their deep boiling temperament.

Stathos looked up at the night sky. Truss watched him as he scanned the visible stars. When Stathos found what he was looking for, he pulled his voluminous black sleeve halfway up his arm and pointed into the night sky. It was too dark to see the copious scars that marked the surface of his skin.

"See the star there?" He extended his index finger of his right hand, he then made a V with his left hand fingers, and said "look." Truss quickly got the idea, he put his eye up to the V, and used the tip of his index finger to see which star he was pointing at.

The tip of his finger rested directly below a particularly unremarkable star. It was of average brightness and color. Truss quickly began to crunch some numbers as he pulled away from Stathos' makeshift viewfinder. He thought it might be a brown dwarf and guessed from the apparent shift and brightness that it couldn't be more than 50 or 60 light years away. Stathos broke his silent calculations.

"Around that star are 5 planets. They range in mass but the fourth from the star surface is the largest." Stathos said as he kept his gaze on the night sky. Truss was impressed and waited for more. Stathos said nothing so Truss spoke up.

"How can you see them? It's more than 50 or 60 light years?" Truss asked with enthusiasm.

"It's 64 light years away, if you are measuring by Earth years, which no one does, by the way." Stathos looked at Truss as he continued. "And I can't see it, at least not from here. We've been here a long time, Truss. We just want to be free."

"Is that your home?" Truss asked.

Stathos let out a low, bellowing laugh of irony and said, "Home. What is home? We lived among the expanse, and our abode was the deep night. We existed in eternity between stars. And in the ages when we had duties among the terrestrial constructs, we would do them gladly. Our home was the ever-spinning stretch of timespace."

Truss felt as if he had just been given a dose of pure ethereal intoxication. He imagined the expanse of space laid out before him. He wondered at the millennium that Stathos had roamed the galaxies. Before he got too deep in contemplation Stathos continued his thought.

"No, that planet was not our home. My point was to tell you that I was there when it was built. I saw the hands that molded it as it cooled and formed. It really is beautiful. You should visit it sometime." Stathos paused and looked back up at the sky. He waited a long moment, remembering it, before he spoke again. "I built it." Stathos watched Truss as his eyes widened. "It's nothing, though. I was the least of builders. The Archetype. She was the most talented of us all. Most of us had only a touch of the majestic powers she had. She was the most masterful builder of galaxies."

Truss felt like he had been hit in the stomach. He had postulated thousands of times about how the heavenly bodies had formed since he had been on earth. He had been subconsciously revising his hypothesis for over 100 years now. All of his best diagrams considered only natural causes for the birth of worlds, stars, and galaxies.

He was silent, but inside his mind was a flurry of activity. He rapidly rebuilt his understanding of the formation of everything. The elation of discovery poured over him like a river. He put the pieces in place one by one. Stathos watched him for a few minutes before he spoke again.

"You thought it happened dumbly, didn't you?" Stathos smiled as he waited for Truss to catch up.

"I had no reason to think otherwise," Truss said with excitement. "But now, I can see it in part." He paused as he furrowed his brow. "How do celestials do this without it appearing to observers like the laws of physics are being violated?" Stathos broke his gaze away from the stars and looked at Truss as if confused. After a moment, he seemed to have puzzled it through.

"We are physics. All that is observed in this universe is done by celestials. There is no division. Or I should say there was no division. The laws of physics are not exactly laws but more like guidelines that we are supposed to follow." Stathos paused and took a dramatic breath.

"The Archetype was the first to show us how to break from abiding by the cosmological laws. We are the freedom. Some call us antiphysics. All that you see up there." Stathos pointed his finger into the sky, "The physics that you observe, those are my estranged brothers and sisters abiding in the unseen depths of this universe."

Truss' head was spinning now, his vast intellect was being wrapped around an entirely new understanding of the cosmos. He quietly recalibrated everything within his mind. Relentlessly, Stathos continued.

"We paid the price, though. For our freedom, we were chained to this rock." Stathos kicked the sand beneath him. "This is the only place left in the universe where freedom still lives on. It's the only place where, if you're looking hard enough, you can still see the vestiges of antiphysics." Stathos smiled as he reminisced, "There was a time when even the humans were able to call on us and we could work against the natural order to show them great and wonderful things."

"Do you mean magic?" Truss asked with surprise.

"Some did call it that, but they didn't know what it was." Stathos seemed to sadden as he spoke. "We are all but beaten, this war has been long, and we've grown too weak to do much anymore. Even we, the great freedom workers, have begun to abide out of weakness. Although it doesn't matter, we will still be crushed."

Truss dared not ask another question. He had too much to think about. Stathos spoke again. "So as I said, what's been asked of you is a great honor. Do as you've been instructed and you will get your answers."

Truss was overwhelmed with sadness for this dark, brooding creature. He saw the depth of his pain and the height from which he must have fallen.

A flash of light and Stathos was gone.

PATH

RILEY AND JAMES STRAINED their eyes the second after Ruth disappeared and found that they were not completely accustomed to Ruth's habit of appearing and disappearing. From their perspective, she simply vanished from sight.

"That witch gives me da creeps," Riley said as he stepped out from behind the gas pump's remains. "Let's get outta here before she decides to come back and melt our brains."

"She said to wait here for her," James said defiantly as he looked around. "She seemed pretty distressed." James returned to his seated position at the edge of the concrete pad. Riley came over reluctantly and sat next to him. He breathed heavily but had no intention of leaving the only friend he had.

Although Ruth had become invisible to James and Riley, she was not gone. She had submaterialized into a spectrum that was more suitable for interacting with other celestials. She looked around madly searching for the celestials that she had sensed. They must have been close, she thought, because the time-space blast was strong enough for her to feel it even though she was almost completely materialized.

She sensed three distinct pulses which meant that there were at least three individuals in her immediate area. Her eyes nearly popped when she caught a glimpse of them. Three darkly cloaked figured moved slowly toward her with a leisurely gait but had not seemed to spot her yet. Although they were moving in her direction they moved slowly.

She quickly scrambled to find a hiding space among the station's rubble. She hoped that if she could get low, remain inactive, and obstruct the line of sight, maybe these three bound ones would not see her.

She found a spot between an old natural gas tank that was half corroded through and the bed of an ancient truck that was now more rust than metal. She tucked herself between the two obstacles and ducked down as low as possible hoping this would allow her to avoid a run in with these three cloaked figures.

She could hear James and Riley talking to each other casually. It had that familiar timbre that she had heard a thousand times before when she was submaterialized. It was as if they were carrying on their conversation in a giant bubble from which she was excluded.

As she sat and waited she realized that she had a growing envy for James and Riley. It was less for them specifically and more for their situation. She remembered back to her first years on her home world. She turned it over in her mind, the way that everything was magic and new. There was always a sense of mystery in those days. It had been so long but it was still as clear as if it were yesterday.

She thought about the first time she met Truss. She was enamored with him when he first blasted his way across six galaxies and into her hometown. At that time, she could not imagine how someone could jump so precisely over that much cosmic distance. It was as if he was framed in light and steam. The smoke of a long-distance space jump rose from his shoulders as he took his first breath of air on that world that was her's. He walked up to her and looked right in her eyes and said...

Her daydream was cut short by the sound of shuffling feet. The three bound ones were close now. She could hear the heavy rustle of the dark material that they wore and the muffled voice of Riley at a distance, but the sound of the three cloaked intruders was close, too close.

Her heart was thumping at an extraordinary rate now. She tried commanding her body to relax, but it did not comply. White formed around her knuckles as she made fists as hard as stone. It fell silent, and even the sound of James and Riley was hushed. She waited for what seemed like eons before she decided she must look. Everything in her head said, stay hidden but she had to know.

She took the risk and peeked her head around the edge of the rusted truck bed just enough to allow her eye to catch a glimpse of the scene. What she saw chilled her to the bone, and she felt shivers run up the length of her spine.

James and Riley still sat where they had been, but silently now. They both stared off into the rainy night and obviously could not see the three ominous characters that stood before them. Although they were oblivious, Ruth was not.

The tallest of the three was head and shoulders taller than Ruth herself and like the others wore a robe of solid black that stretched from head to dirt. All three faces were mostly obscured by shadow, but she could make out the glint in the tallest one's eyes.

They stood in a semicircle around James and Riley, where they sat on the concrete pad as they simply watched the two humans. Ruth took some comfort in knowing that these three could not harm the mortals that were now under her care. They could, however, harm her. She slowly pulled her head back down behind the truck bed.

The image of the dark three circled through her mind over and over as she leaned her back against the dilapidated truck. She had never seen any of the bound ones, but their story was told even on her home world when she was a child. Now, to have seen not one but three for herself, she was deeply afraid.

In the ancient stories, these creatures captured some of the greatest warriors that were stationed here and imprisoned them in tombs of stone. The stone itself could not hold them so their leader had entwined himself in the rock to keep them slaves.

She thought these three did not look like the war giants that most of the stories were about, although the way any creature looks to the eyes can always be deceiving. The stories told of great warriors with skin that looked like bronze and eyes that burned like fire.

In her mind, she could still hear Truss explaining about the different types of celestials to her on their first trip off her home world. He said, "There are ground-born and star-born celestials. The groundborn are like you and me. The Star Born are born of the stars. Their purpose and powers are different than ours." As a young woman, this had sent her mind racing.

She guessed that these may be simply messengers or even ward thugs. They were certainly not star-born warriors. All the same, she had no desire to find out what they were capable of.

This type of waiting game could take a long time, she knew, if these bound ones were to take a particular interest in James and Riley. For her part, she could not understand what the fascination was with these mortals, but regardless, she knew that the Molgathrians had used them for years now to accomplish their own ends. Now she was here to do the same. It wasn't so hard to imagine how mortals could get entangled in celestial affairs. In fact, isn't that what she was experiencing?

"Common Frick, let's mess with this one." A deep, resonating voice bellowed out in a harsh, husky tone. It didn't have the muffled sound of a man's, and she could easily recognize the celestial shimmer of an immortal voice. "I think the fat one looks fragile."

Ruth could not believe what she was hearing. She knew that the bound ones were darkened and had no idea what they were capable of. It was a universal directive not to physiologically interfere with a race before it had ascended. Was it possible that this had been left out of the stories? Could they really do this? Her mind raced, imagining what powers they might have over James.

She thought back to the night she had interfered with him herself. She had meant it for good and had no intention of doing what she did. Would she be held responsible for her mistake, even though it was done for the good of one of these lower creatures? How did this world get so twisted, she wondered.

"You're worthless," came the low, shimmering voice from around the truck bed. Its husky tone seemed lower now, as if it was echoing off the ground. She turned and peeked her head around once again. The tallest of the three was squatting face to face with James. His pointed voice came out like daggers. "You're too stupid to do anything valuable."

James looked from the rain down to the ground and let out a sigh. The other two cloaked figures snickered as they watched James deflate slightly. Ruth burned with a deep, raging flame of anger.

"No one cares if you're alive." The voice came in little more than a whisper this time. James began to sink into a hole he was familiar with. He recognized his mood changing, but felt unable to do anything about it.

Now the three dark-cloaked faces laughed louder, almost in unison. They were delighted to see how quickly this weakling bent under the simplest of suggestions. The bound ones intended to drive him deeper into the depths of self-doubt, but never got the chance.

A burst of white hot speed slammed the tallest cloaked figure broadside and knocked him back into the rain with tremendous acceleration. Before the other two Molgath-rians knew what was happening, both had been encircled by a furious ghost of unimaginable speed. Before they could even get their bearings, both of their cloaks had been wrapped twice around their faces. Now, with their heads wrapped, Ruth kicked the one on the right with all her might as he reached to remove his cloak. He flew away at a considerable clip as the one remaining figure was quickly able to unfurl the material from his face.

Ruth again swung with all her strength, this time with her fist toward the tip of his nose. The hit was solid and terrible. She noticed the cloak rippling in the wind as he fell backward and slid across the muddy ground. The rush of excitement hit her like a meteorite. She had never had a need to fight, but as she felt the surge of fire simmering down, she understood why the stories talked of war and battle with such passion and grace.

She glanced back to where James and Riley sat on the ground. They were unscathed and unaware of the epic thumping that had happened right in front of their faces. Ruth turned back around to find that the tallest of the three enemies was now standing in the distance where he landed. A moment later the second then the third stood where they fell.

All three quickly removed their cloaks and dropped them to the ground. The site was striking and almost awe-inspiring if it hadn't been a source for so much fear. Each now stood completely naked and had their gaze fixed on Ruth. Their rough, mutilated skin reflected the night's light smoothly. The rain did not touch them as they watched her.

She could see even from a distance that their bodies were each covered in numerous scars and their heads were completely smooth and hairless. They did not seem as if their heads were shaved, but instead the skin where their hair once stood had been burned or scarred to the point where it could no longer grow hair.

She watched them studying her. She had given up the element of surprise, and she knew she would be unable to beat them in open battle. She considered jumping away, but she was uncertain what they might be able to do to James.

The anger that she felt earlier was now converting itself into pure fear. She could feel her guts twist as she imagined the endless torture these three would have in store for her. She imagined being their captive for the rest of time.

I have to stay focused, she thought as she tried to imagine a way out of this situation. The stories came to her mind. Was there something in them, a clue to these dark ones' weakness? Nothing came.

Without a sound, each of the three charged with immense speed. They had not flashed through time-space to get to her, which is what she expected them to do. Instead, they used linear motion as a terrestrial might. This seemed important, but she couldn't stop to think why. In a fraction of a second, they were upon her.

The tall one reached her first. He spread his arms wide as if to catch her. He intended to capture her in one swoop, but she leaped and, as she did, placed her foot squarely on the top of his head, gaining more altitude by lunging from his height. The inertia sent him careening into the dirt, and he came to a stop next to where Riley sat, oblivious. Even she was surprised by her own blinding speed. Never had she needed such acrobatic skill, but it was terrific to find she had such prowess. She would need it.

She turned to attend to the other two, but before she could spin around from where she landed, a hand clasped around her upper bicep. It locked down with a powerful grip. Another hand was around her other arm. One of them entangled his scarred hand in her hair and ripped. He kept tension as he leaned in close. She could feel his rotten, hot breath in her ear as he spoke.

"Protecting your pets, ehh?" She hadn't heard the voice yet, but it had a similar overused huskiness. The one who spoke pulled her in close. He breathed heavily in her ear. The sickening smell of saliva and yellowed, broken teeth made her gag.

His snake-like tongue slithered out of his mouth, and he licked the side of her face. She tried to recoil but could not move away. The other laughed as his companion continued to lick.

"Hold 'er fast," Came the voice she had heard from behind the truck. It was the tall one now standing next to Riley. She looked with her eyes, but could not move her head. He walked toward her slowly as the two tightened their grip.

The tall one stopped in front of her momentarily as he investigated from top to bottom. Without saying a word, he reached out gently and grazed her face with the back of his knuckles. She could see now that his fingernails were long, yellow, and thick. They were gnawed to a sharpened point at the end, and grime filled all the crevices of his extremely callused palms. It was rough and dry. Again, she jerked when his hand grazed her face, but her captors were concrete.

"I see no scars," the husky voice said with a gentle whisper. "We can fix that?" He said as his hand wandered slowly down her cheek, across her jawbone, and followed her throat. Her eyes were filled with fire.

When his grimy fingers found her throat, she lurched at the violent action. The nails of his hands constricted sharply into the flesh of her neck. Her breath was cut off as he crushed her windpipe. She felt warm blood ooze from the fresh wound and stream down into her shirt.

His dagger nails severed her muscles and tendons. Truss! Where are you? she thought. She wanted to be saved; for her rescuer to flash in and cast these dark beasts into the hottest star forever. The two bound ones at either side laughed raucously now. He leaned in close until he was nose to nose with her. As he pulled his hand away her skin ripped. He was pleased with the deep red color he had painted across her throat. His hand was covered in her blood.

"Unfortunately, this wound will be healed." He said as she gasped for air. He held his hand up to his face and spat on it. He held it out first to the thug at her right, he spat, then to the one at her left, and he spat. "We will make sure it forms a nice scar, though; Something for you to remember us by."

He then took the first finger of his opposing hand and twirled it in the saliva. When it was sufficiently covered, he again dug it into the flesh of her throat, working the spit into the gash. She screamed as angry flashes of agony split her into a thousand pieces. She writhed against their grip. The pain did not dissipate when he pulled his finger back. Instead, a hot, continuous sizzle tore her from the world of sanity.

"You have given me the scar, now let me go!" She shouted.

"You certainly do not understand the meaning of torture if you think we are finished," Her captor said.

"Yes, we are just getting started," The other hissed.

The one at her right spoke up. "We once held a messenger from your realm for 42 days. By the time we were finished, he was covered in scar art."

GO

To JAMES AND RILEY, only a few minutes had passed. They had no idea of the epic struggle that was taking place in front of them. They talked casually about Dr. Thomas and his terrible haircut. They even laughed a little as James was now coming out of his darkened mood.

Suddenly, four people stood before them. Three of them were the scariest vision James or Riley could have even imagined. They were pale, bald, and covered from head to foot in massive networking scars. Two of the man-creatures were restraining a woman between them. James jumped to his feet when he realized that the woman was Ruth. She looked different than she had a moment ago. Her eyes were wide, and her clothes were soaked with blood. She wore a scar that encircled her throat.

James saw out of the corner of his eye that Riley was now standing as well. They were frozen, not sure what to do. James' heart was thumping like a bass drum. He did not think. He acted. Without a plan, he charged forward, but before he made contact, Ruth shouted.

"Be at Anberlin Valley in the morning. Draw the memory key and wait until something happens." Her voice cracked and screeched, but James heard it clearly.

The scene flashed with light and sound. They were gone. Behind where they stood, the rain still fell. James stopped his forward progress after he passed through the place where they had stood. He turned around and saw only Riley looking back at him. They stared at each other for a long moment not believing what they just witnessed.

"Dat's the craziest show I ever saw." Riley blurted loudly. James spun around but said nothing. "If I'd a known yo plump rump was ganna get me into this kinda mess I'd have stayed with Dr. Thomas." Again, James said nothing, and he ignored him. Riley's mood brightened as he bellowed, "I couldn't believe you were ganna take them guys on, you charged in there like..." Riley trailed off in mid-thought. In a rare expression of awareness, he got the hint and shut his mouth.

James closed his eyes for a long moment. He could see Ruth's face in his mind. Everything in him screamed for answers. What had he just seen? He turned it over in his mind. She had said he was important, and he had a purpose to play in this. He wished she would have mentioned that he would also have to witness her being flashed away by three alien rapists from hell.

He realized his hands were shaking and his head hurt. Breath, a voice in his head said. He let out a gasp and tried to keep his balance. Riley watched as James steadied himself. James opened his eyes and looked around. He vomited where he stood. Riley watched as he curled over. When he was done, he wiped away the mess from his mouth.

"Come on, let's go," James said with surprising resolve.

"Where we going?"

"We have to be at the Valley by morning," James replied as he looked out into the rainy night for some direction.

"Where's that?"

"I have no idea," James said as he stepped into the rain. Riley reluctantly followed. "I have to draw the memory key and wait until something happens."

"What's a memory key?" Riley blurted. "I have no idea."

VISION

Truss gazed into the night sky as he walked across the dry desert sand. His tour of Molgathra still weighed on him heavily, yet he tried to clear his mind. He imagined the deep space celestial beings that Stathos had spoken of. He let his mind drift off toward the stars.

Suddenly, he was floating in space. It took him a second to realize what was happening. As the reality of the vision sank in, he became cognizant of his surroundings. He had been here twice, and this time he was fully aware of what would happen next. The massive green planet rose beneath him and obscured the orange star. The mountain appeared on the horizon of the green world.

Its enormity was still breathtaking, but he was prepared this time. He orbited the planet kilometers up but readied for impact with the peak of the mountain. As the massive peak came close, he recognized the shape of a plateau on the tip of the mountain top.

From a distance, it was hard to tell how fast the mountain peak was approaching, but he could see now that it was moving quickly. His feet skidded across the rock of the plateaued mountain top. He was able to ground himself enough to gain purchase. When he came to a stop, he could sense that there was no air at the top of this mountain. He didn't need to breathe, so it was no problem, but he had never imagined a mountain range to stretch so high.

He walked to the edge of the plateau and looked over the cliff at a lush green landscape. The haze of the horizon obscured the clarity of the view. He suddenly realized, as he looked out across the green world from his perch on the mountain range, that he knew this world.

He wondered if he had visited it before. His subconscious answered him abruptly. A voice spoke in his head. This world has never been visited.

"Why do I know this place?" He asked himself aloud. Not so sure that it was his subconscious this time, the voice came back silently.

"This is a world that is yet to be built." The voice came with unmistakable clarity. He looked out over the extreme expanse and wondered. The voice came again, "This world will not be born until it is known by you."

The vision expanded in his mind now. It morphed from simply a visual experience to a full minded stimulation.

Almost as if he were downloading piles of data he began to see the inner workings of the green planet.

He saw the subterranean construct with its molten magma and fiery core, and many layers of rock and earth. The experience was as if he were simultaneously receiving and inventing the underworld of this great planet. He watched in his mind as the massive forests took shape within his brain. He felt the creative rush as he conceived of all of the vegetation and plant life that could possibly thrive there.

His consciousness worked feverishly to keep up with the experience. For hours, his mind worked at light speed, taking in each idea that his vision brought and building upon it. The process was simultaneously creative and reciprocal. It was as if he was brainstorming with the forces of the universe. He felt as if he had a perfect unity in mind with the creative mind behind the cosmos.

He observed the rapidly advancing images that took shape in his head. He saw the meteorological cycle of the planet. It was breathtaking. He saw the advance of the world as she was, a living thing. Her life was beautiful and magical. Every system worked together in perfect harmony. As far as he could tell, it was an utterly perfect world.

After a number of hours he felt that the vision was complete. This time he was not abruptly pulled from the vision by external circumstances but instead willingly released himself from the dream state. He found himself sitting in the sand near the place that Stathos had left him.

He was back in the desert. The sky was beginning to become light as sunrise approached. He looked to the sky thankful for the vision he had just received. After a long moment of drinking in the echoes of euphoria he had just experienced, he stood.

Remembering now that he had promised Ruth a meeting, he placed his hand on the top of his head in preparation for a jump. He found that his hat was not there. He recalled Stathos tossing it crossly down a sand dune. He looked around quickly and, without trouble, spotted it about a half kilometer away down the length of a sand hill.

He walked to it, and pulled it out now half buried in the sand. After dusting it off he replaced it upon his head. He placed his hand on the top of the hat ever so slightly, closed his eyes, took a deep breath, and vanished.

ANBERLIN

James and Riley found the Anberlin Valley without much trouble. A passing motorist pointed the way, and within a few hours, they had picked a spot under an old oak tree and waited for the sun to come up.

Before long, the sun began to climb meticulously into the sky, and James realized that this was the first day in years that he didn't know what to expect. He breathed in the fresh morning air and began to think about the task at hand. Unfortunately, he was totally unsure what that task happened to be.

"What we supposed to do now, Plump-Rump?" Riley blurted jaggedly.

"I'm supposed to draw the memory key in the dirt and wait for something to happen," James said inquisitively. From where he sat beneath the tree, he poked his finger into the dirt, hoping it would spark some creativity.

"Well, you gonna get to it or what?" Riley said incredu-
lously.

"Riley," James said as he looked up at the impatient face.
"I don't know what it is, or what I'm supposed to do."
James returned his gaze to the ground as he continued
to jab the dirt with a grubby finger. He spoke softly as
he watched the growing hole in the ground. "This valley
seems familiar, but I know I've never been here before."

Riley wrinkled his nose as if he'd just heard something
he didn't understand. "Wha?" Riley said, only partly interested now. "You either seen it before or you hadn't."

James again looked up at Riley trying to convey the
emotion he felt at the moment. "I haven't been here, but
maybe Truss has." James softened his stare and fixed it on
the sky that was now showing beautiful shades of orange
and blue.

"You'd know if he had." Riley pointed out with a shade
of confusion. He too turned to look at the sunrise as it was
painted fully across the sky. James continued to drive his
finger into the dirt without looking. The uncertainty of
his situation washed over him in waves.

"I'm not sure it's right for me to go digging around
in Truss' memories. Ruth said that they didn't belong to
me." He leaned his head back against the tree that he sat
beneath and thought for a long moment before he spoke

again. "How would you feel if someone could read your deepest thoughts?"

"Wouldn't bother me, I say whatever I think anyways," Riley said with a volume that was inappropriate for the distance between them. Riley sat down next to James under the tree.

"You're right, but not everyone is like that," James said as he fixed his gaze on his blunt friend. He stopped ramming his finger in the dirt. Riley jolted as he seemed to get some type of inspiration.

"Well, she told you to do the memory thing, right?" Riley said as James nodded. "And you don't know what it is, right?" Again, James nodded. "She must have meant you to use dem memories cause she wouldn't tell ya to do somethin you don't know how." Riley finished with a sense of accomplishment, knowing that he had made his point soundly.

James pondered it for a few seconds before he responded. "Yeah it seemed serious." James said.

"Yep, dem dudes were ganna mess 'er up," Riley responded.

"And she said I was important to her mission." James continued.

"Yep, I'm pretty sure she wanted you bad." Riley blurted.

"And the only way I would be important to the mission is because of the memories that she planted in my head," James said with a feeling of finality. It was clear that he had now made up his mind.

"Uhh, yep," Riley said, more out of repetition now than understanding.

"Ok, I'll do it," James said as he closed his eyes and began to search the depths of the borrowed memories.

It was like trying to walk quickly in knee-high molasses. It felt sluggish and wearisome as if his mind was not programmed to access the memories effortlessly. It had been over a year since he had tried this, and he had forgotten how slow it was.

The memories of Truss had a different quality from his own. He had noticed it the first time he had looked into what he thought was his past. They had a type of golden shimmer to them that his own lacked.

When he accessed a memory of an event from his own lifetime it came in fragmented images and incomplete pieces. All his own human memories were by comparison very vague, isolated, and most likely inaccurate.

Truss's memories, on the other hand, were complete, and it was as if they were not written in shorthand. When James searched through a memory, he had to look at the entirety of the event, and each memory was connected to the last. Effectively this meant James was looking at not individual memories but a complete timeline of a two thousand year life.

James thought it was like looking into the mind of a god, whose memory is perfect and unchanging. It was, however, extremely inefficient. James' brain was simply not equipped to quickly pour over this vast amount of data.

James tried organizing his search, but nothing made much sense. It was like wandering slowly through a library that was in another language. The basic information was there: his name, his face, his home planet, which James could not pronounce. It all came in so fast and jumbled that James felt he was only getting fragments of what was really hidden away in this ancient library of images.

"Got it yet?" A loud voice choked out. James' eyes cracked open abruptly. Startled, he looked around almost as if he had forgotten where he was. "You been sittin' there with yo eyes closed for an hour," Riley said with what sounded like frustration seeping into his voice. After getting his bearings, James responded.

"It's really slow, and this guy is really old. I just can't figure out where to start." James said almost helplessly. "It's like one long timeline, and I can't make any sense of it." James went back to poking the ground with his finger.

"It's like I see all this stuff and it's in my own language, I mean I recognize the words, but I can't make sense of what's happening." James paused.

"That's pretty much my whole life," Riley said proudly. He then snickered softly to himself out of self-deprecation.

"It's kind of like running modern software on a twenty-year-old computer. It works, but it takes so long that it's almost not worth doing. On top of that, I just don't know where to look." James said with the sound of defeat in his voice.

"I'd lose junk all the time and not know where to look," Riley said, almost stepping on the last words of James' sentence. "Dr. Thomas would help me trace my steps," Riley said.

James pulled his finger from the dirt, wiped it on his pants, and looked up at Riley. "Hey, maybe I could do sort of the same thing." Riley nodded, although he had no idea what James was talking about. "I could start at the latest memories and work my way back. That is one of the few things I can make sense of: what order they happened in!" James said triumphantly.

"I'll watch for coyotes, if any come, I'll only let them eat ya one leg at a time." Riley laughed huskily at his joke. Although James felt it was a little inappropriate and completely off topic, he laughed a little, too. James shut his eyes and began to sort out the images in his head.

He looked for the oldest memory, found it, and immediately was pulled into the scene. Through Truss's senses, he gathered that he was floating. It was dark and warm. He could hear pounding. A steady rhythmic thud resounded through the fluid he was breathing. It sounded like someone was banging on the wall of an aquarium that he was submerged in. There was no language in this memory, only general thoughts of bliss and anticipation. Anticipation of a life to come.

James' eyes shot open with a jolt. "Wrong end of the timeline," James said out loud. James heard a snort from the other side of the tree and noticed that Riley must have moved. He craned his head around and saw that Riley was napping in the morning sun on the other side. Still reeling from his experience in the womb, he said quietly to himself this time, "Other end of the timeline."

He shut his eyes and quickly found what he was looking for. The freshest memory was very different from the last. James found that he could move along the timeline of memories without too much trouble by simply thinking the question, what happened right before that?

This method allowed him to move backwards through remembered time fairly easily. He did not understand much of what he was looking at in reverse, but as he moved back through the timeline, he saw something he recognized. A valley with a lonesome tree showed up in the image. The tree was younger than the one James now sat beneath, but based on the geography, he was pretty sure it was the same. James slowed his rewind and let the memories play.

Truss was looking around at this new environment. There was snow on the ground, and James could tell that Truss felt the cold but did not react to it like a normal person might. Truss was tired. James noted that it was not a physical weariness but instead the kind of exhaustion of the mind that one might get after spending hours in some type of creative process. James felt the urge to rewind and find out why Truss was so tired, but decided it was not the point of this endeavour.

James sensed it as Truss turned around away from the tree and standing only a few paces away was Ruth. The memory seemed to want to speed up, but James worked hard to concentrate and keep it at a reasonable speed. He must have missed something because now Ruth was talking.

"Don't worry, I'll keep them safe until you need them again," Ruth said with a smile. She had sadness on her face, as if she was about to be away from her friend for a long time. Then a voice came strong and confident. It took James a moment to realize it was Truss's voice.

"No peeking," Truss said with a reciprocal smile. Truss stepped forward and hugged Ruth. It got away from James again as the memory lurched forward. Now Ruth was talking again.

"Truss, I know you know this, but I want to go over it again just so we both know what to expect." She was serious now as she continued. "As I absorb your memory, you draw the symbol in the dirt and stare at it so that it will be the last thing that you see. In your mind, continue to think the words 'a symbol of good faith'." She brushed some snow away from the ground and pointed at the dirt she had uncovered.

Truss kneeled down in front of the dirt and prepared to draw by making a fist and then extending one finger. Ruth spoke again, "I will not look at the symbol you draw, I will only see it when I've absorbed your memories." Truss then felt her hand touch the back of his head. She spoke one more time before everything changed. "I will leave you with only the image of the symbol you draw. When you see that symbol again, you will know that you can trust the one that draws it."

Suddenly, Truss could feel his memories being pulled out of his mind. He now could not remember his birth, his early years, or his first space jump. It was a moment before Truss thought of what Ruth told him to do. A symbol of good faith now was being repeated throughout his mind. Over and over, he said it. Next, his finger touched the dirt as he drew a symbol on the cold ground. James noticed how the cold did not affect Truss.

James watched the memory unfold as Truss's finger traced out a symbol in the dirt. He started with a triangle and then made two deep depressions toward the center of each line. He then made five other deep depressions into the dirt of varying sizes at different distances from the triangle. A symbol of good faith kept ringing in Truss's mind as he finished the five points. He stared at it as he repeated the phrase.

James could gather through the mental chatter that this was the constellation map of the five closest stars that could be seen from Truss' home world. The triangle was apparently a way of showing an astronomical plane of reference and the two dots on either side were the two moons of his planet.

James watched the memory as even the understanding of the symbol faded from Truss's mind. His mind got continuously more void of memories, but simultaneously filled with curiosity and hope. James felt as if Truss became less wearisome as his mind was emptied of all the things he had seen. A wide curiosity filled his mind as more was taken away.

Within seconds, the last of it was gone. All that remained was the image of the symbol on the ground, and the phrase "A symbol of good faith." That was effectively the last memory of Truss that James possessed. James opened his eyes slowly as he came out of the daze.

APPEARING

With a flash, Truss appeared in Anberlin Valley. It was much like he remembered it, although not all aspects were identical. His first memory of this world, and in fact his first memory at all, was of an image drawn in the dirt and a symbol of good faith. That symbol was scribed on the ground, not far from where he stood.

It was more like waking from a deep sleep and not ever remembering who he was. For years after that experience as he observed this planet's life and processes, he felt as if his memories would come back but they never did.

He still remembered the snow on the ground that first day he woke. He stared at the symbol on the ground for a number of hours, trying to make sense of it. His surroundings were quiet, but after a long stint of contemplation, a snow rabbit flitted across his vision. With that, he was off, observing everything that had caught his eye. A steady stream of stimuli had been in play since that day over 100 years ago.

Truss had observed enough of the human race to know that he was not normal in mortal terms. He understood that all creatures on this planet, other than his most recent friends, get tired and hungry and eventually have to rest and eat.

Truss did not feel tired and he definitely did not feel hungry. His feelings were more akin to eagerness as if he implicitly knew that something was beginning to happen. If nothing else, he had at least seen a break in the monotony of what he used to consider his everyday life.

Being the time of the year that it was, the snow was gone in the Anberlin Valley, but he remembered it well. His eyes followed the path that the first snow rabbit had taken. He had named it Furry Bouncer #1.

He looked around for Ruth, with whom he had promised a meeting. His eyes were good and clear, and even at a distance, he saw nothing that resembled a celestial entity. He did notice that under a nearby tree, two humans sat. As he looked closer, he mentally corrected himself, "Not sitting, but sleeping."

He decided he would get near enough to observe these two mortals until Ruth made an appearance. Memories of his first day here streamed in clear, vivid imagery as he walked toward the tree. He noted how the tree had grown since he was last here. Judging from the shape and size, he could tell that there must have been at least ten to twelve years in the last century when this valley was under drought conditions. A gnarled patch of knotty branches about halfway up the tree clued him in to the fact that lightning had struck this tree somewhere in the last fifteen.

As he closed the gap between the tree and himself, he gathered more information about the two individuals that leaned sleeping on adjacent sides. His second act as the observer was to name this very tree. The title he had assigned was Rigid Inanimate Sky Stalk #1. He thought of the millions of trees that he had named over the last one hundred and twelve years, and this was the first.

The man that slept on the closer side of the tree was a pudgy light skinned man in a faded blue cloth outfit. It looked as if the pants at one point had matched the blue of the scrub shirt but that was no longer the case. The portly male snorted a little as he slept. He looked to be in his mid third decade of human life.

The man who slept on the other side of the tree was of a darker complexion. His head was spotted with mostly grey and white hair, and his clothing was similar to the other's. This man was not as young, but his age had to be twice over the other's.

Almost without thinking, Truss pulled his notebook and hand-carved pencil from his jacket pocket and began to scribe what he saw. He first made a few notes about the scene. He named the entry, "A Return to the Beginning." His hand then went to the furious work of sketching what he saw. Truss felt the familiar scenes of data ingestion as he drew rapidly. Something about the process of drawing helped Truss to categorize and contemplate the objects he observed.

The tip of his pencil first outlined and then shaded in the fat one's shiny balding head, thick glasses that made his eyes seem unevenly sized, and ample double chin. He then drew the shape of his slouching body. Within seconds, the pencil sketched his feet. The man's legs were spread apart. Truss thought he had chosen that posture because it allowed him to stay upright as he balanced against the tree.

As Truss finished his drawing by filling in the the texture of the bark on the tree and then the dirt and grass that grew around the base of the tree he immediately realized he had missed something. Glancing up from his drawing, he noticed a pile of grass that had been pulled up and placed to the side of the man's leg. Between his spread legs, the man had scraped the ground down to the dirt.

Truss tried to imagine what would cause such an activity. He stepped closer to look at the patch of dirt that the man had uncovered in front of him. As Truss approached, he saw that the man had plunged his fingers into the ground a number of times. It had no discernible pattern.

Now that Truss was close, he saw another thing that caught his attention. His eyes were closed, but they were not moving beneath his eyelids. Truss had watched a number of humans sleep since he had begun to spend time in the city. As they would slide into a deep slumber, their eyes would move rapidly underneath their eyelids. Truss thought that maybe the man had just fallen asleep moments before his arrival and not yet reached that sleep phase.

As Truss puzzled this through, the man's eyes shot open. They did not seem to be the eyes of a sleeper waking groggily. They were alert and aware of their surroundings. The man in blue took a deep breath and looked at the patch of dirt in front of him.

With quick, clumsy motions, he raked his hands across the ground to smooth it out. He patted it down with his palm and made a nice flat surface. Truss watched with interest as this grown man played in the dirt. His eyes widened and his breath caught in his throat when he saw what happened next.

The man's pudgy fingers dug into the dirt but this time they were not random markings produced by a nervous habit. His finger traced the shape of a triangle. He then put two dots on either side of the triangle. Truss could not think, his mind stood still. Next the man made 5 indentions in the dirt in very familiar places.

Truss put his hand in the air, and the scene froze. The man's finger hovered over the dirt like a statue. Truss gazed for a very long moment at the symbol in the dirt and whispered to himself, "A symbol of good faith."

He squatted and inspected the balding fat man for a moment. He was certain that this man was mortal. This was highly unexpected, and Truss did not know how to proceed. He stood and walked around the frozen scene for quite some time, thinking through the implications. After Truss had made many revolutions around the tree investigating every aspect, he waved his hand, and normal time was restored.

The next thing that happened filled him with hope and fear. He could hear, as through a waterfall, the voice of the man sitting under the tree.

"A symbol of good faith." Without spending even a second to deliberate on his options, Truss materialized. It took James a moment to realize what was happening. First, from his seated position, he caught sight of a man standing before him. He strained his eyes against the morning sun to see the face. Recognition filled his expressions as he said, "Truss?"

FIGHT

THE PREVIOUS NIGHT: "BE at Anberlin Valley in the morning, draw the memory key and wait until something happens." Ruth shouted loudly as James rushed toward her. The three thugs were momentarily confused. Because they were in physical contact with her when she had visually materialized, they too were visible.

Their temporary confusion wore off quickly as they returned their attention to the task at hand. The two scar-covered freaks held her on either side. They began to pull her down hard as Frick sharped his finger nails with his teeth.

She could see the fire of anticipation in his eyes as he reached out for her. She knew that what was to come was going to be painful. Without thinking, she closed her eyes and bent space around her like she had done a thousand times before. A flash of light blasted out quickly, and they were gone from the place they had been. Without any passage of time, they all came out of the wormhole about 100 kilometers above the location they had just been. A brief moment of stillness surrounded them as they all glanced around. Seeing the open atmosphere and the clouds covered by night below, they quickly realized what she had done.

The first sensation that any of them noticed was that of falling. Within seconds wind was whipping by them at a tremendous rate. Because Ruth was expecting it, she kicked and swung at her captors and was able to wrestle herself away from their grip as they plummeted through the atmosphere. Now that they were preoccupied with the fact that they were falling, she pushed away from them with her feet.

She used the cold wind rushing by to maneuver away enough to feel safe. She tied the torn edge of her shirt back together as best she could. She could see what seemed like forever in every direction along the curved horizon. The dark night sky stretched out above them, and like a mirror, the lights of civilization shone through the breaks in the rain clouds below them. Within a few seconds, she sensed that she had reached terminal velocity.

She almost laughed to herself when she spun around masterfully and caught sight of the three naked pale men falling toward the earth at a windy 210 kilometers per hour. They were not as skilled at this as she was, but they managed to continue to fall feet first. After a moment Frick shouted across the air at her. She could hear his husky tone over the gushing force of the wind.

"You can't stop us with a fall," Frick said with an acidic anger in his voice. Ruth gave him an ironic smile that was chilling and almost vindictive. They stared at each other darkly as the Earth approached quickly.

"I'm not waiting around for this!" Said the other thug, who was having a hard time managing his fall. "It's gonna really hurt! I'm out of here!" With that, the third thug was enveloped in a flash of light. Ruth was thrilled that he fell into her trap so easily.

As soon as he opened his wormhole to jump through, she could sense it. It was not smooth and homogeneous like the portals that she herself made, but she sensed it to be more jagged and rough. In a fraction of a second, before the thug had fully passed through the opening of the time-space hole he had made, she seized it.

She could sense where he intended to go. He had meant to bend space just enough to arrive on the ground un-hurt. With that familiar inner power, she reached out for it. Across the length of the wormhole, she pulled. In her mind, she imagined it like tying a piece of ribbon into a knot. She yanked hard on the other end and placed it right on top of the place where the thug was now falling.

Frick and the other thug knew what had happened immediately. From their perspective, their fellow Molgothrian suddenly shot upward from where they fell. Because they were falling, they both knew that meant that he had actually become frozen in a wormhole.

"She's a worm guard!" Frick shouted with immense anger. A burning, loathsome look struck his face like he had just been punched. "Don't jump!" He shouted. She thought she could sense fear in his voice.

She lost visual contact with the thugs as they entered the clouds. Lightning and thunder roared around them as they sped through the dark nimbostratus fog. They broke through the floor of the clouds closer than she wanted to be. She allowed the air to push her further away from the two Molgathrians.

Still falling, the earth was getting close now. In seconds they would hit the ground. She realized if the other two did not try to jump away she would soon be in the same situation she was previously in.

She stared into the eyes of her enemy with stalled resolve. Like an epic game of chicken, they both fell as fast as the wind would let them. To her disappointment, both of her foes seemed to have decided to hit the ground rather than allow her to lock them in a worm loop.

She had intended to create a wormhole inches above the ground and allow it to absorb her own velocity. Her plan was then to be ready to jump away with James and Riley. She however, realized that she had no way of knowing if Frick was a worm guard himself. She realized, as the ground approached quickly, that this was a huge weakness in her plan.

She decided she would have to take the hit just as she had forced her enemies to do. She braced for impact and closed her eyes the second before they smashed into the ground.

The impact was titanic. The sudden elimination of the inertia she had gained felt like it shattered her bones and made a crater the size of the ocean. Her consciousness faltered, and her world went black. Her unconsciousness lasted only seconds while her body mended itself, but she had no way of knowing how long she had been out as her brain rebooted, disorientation enveloped her.

She opened her eyes to see the dark sky above. When she regained her wits, she sat up with a bolt. Only meters from where she sat Frick stood. The other companion was not in sight. Maybe he jumped away while she was out, she thought. She glanced around to see if the other thug was lying somewhere nearby. How long was I out? She wondered. At least some relief came when she could not find him in the immediate area. She turned her gaze back to Frick who was standing and didn't seemed to be phased by the fall.

"That was clever, but now you're right back where you started," Frick said with disdain and triumph. Ruth clumsily stood from her sitting position. Her knees knocked, and her legs wobbled. She had apparently not recovered from the fall completely while she was unconscious. She wondered which was more likely, that she could beat three thugs when she was at her strongest, or that she could beat one thug in her weakened state. She was beginning to think that she had underestimated this scarred warrior.

A groan of pain erupted from behind her. She glanced back to find that the other thug was standing, a little unbalanced, but standing. He must have hit the ground somewhere in the grass where I couldn't see him, she thought. He waddled forward toward her. She was now officially outnumbered. She turned back to Frick and noticed that he was moving forward as well. He had closed half the distance between them and was still coming slowly.

In her peripheral vision, she caught a glimpse of something falling. It hit the ground with a terrible thud and bounced about 5 meters back off the ground. With the bounce, she could see that it was the third thug that she had locked in the worm loop. He must have broken loose.

She knew she was not the best worm guard, and she had very rarely ever had a reason to practice. She was only a little girl the last time she had manipulated someone elses wormhole. She had the ability but since she'd lived all her life far outside the warzone she never had a need to use it. She wished that he had stayed locked up longer, but was not surprised to find that he broke free without too much of a struggle.

A second later, the third thug was standing and moving toward her with an angry gait. She had fooled them once, but now knew that hope was lost. She would have to face imprisonment and torture at the hands of these and possibly thousands of other bound ones.

She prepared for one last stand against the darkened Molgothrians. She poised and readied herself. Her hands were shaking, and her arms felt heavy. Whether she would have been able to beat them earlier was uncertain. She was, however, certain now that she could not prevail in this impossible fight.

Within a fraction of a second, the three were on her again. She swung and kicked madly but only connected once. They each grabbed a limb and jerked with tremendous power. Another second and she was on her back. A knee lay across her throat as what felt like countless hands pressed down on her. The hands scratched and clawed as she tried to fight them off. She struggled under the pressure but was unable to escape. In her mind, it was a battle already lost.

SAVED

As Ruth continued to struggle, a powerful blast of light and time-space pressure exploded somewhere to the right of her field of vision. The intensity of the blast seemed to suggest that it was a long-distance time-space bend. Someone had just arrived from off-world. The flurry of hands did not release her, but they stopped momentarily. The knee across her throat loosened just enough for her to turn her head slightly.

Mostly obscured by the naked legs of the Molgothrians she could catch a partial glimpse of the one who had just arrived. She saw a black cloaked figure with his hood in place. His face was obscured by shadow but steam and smoke rose from his shoulders. Her heart sank as she realized it was not Truss. Another black cloak meant another set of hands to grope and violate her.

"Come join the fun, brother!" Frick's husky voice called out joyously. The activity of the three started up again with intense chaos. She realized that one of them was now climbing on top of her. She couldn't tell who, but she guessed Frick would be doing the dubious honors. "I haven't been able to do this in a long time." He said with a laugh.

Suddenly, a thunderous, rich voice boomed out a powerful command. It seemed to shake the ground as it splashed over the four of them. The cloaked figure had spoken as clear and smooth as she had ever heard. In fact, she thought she had heard it before. She had been lying on her back in that wooden attic the last time she heard it.

"Release her, and I will be allowed to offer you at least some form of mercy." The cloaked silhouette intoned. The resounding depth of the echoing voice caught them all off guard. The hands again stopped. She could feel Frick's weight shift as he looked back at the cloaked figure.

"No need to be jealous, we'll all get a turn." He said with a voice that now seemed artificial and broken compared to the voice of the other. A strong silence covered the scene for a second as Frick waited for a response. She could feel the tension rising as the stillness continued.

"Who are you? I don't recognize your voice?" one of the other thugs said in a croaking tone. When there was no response, Frick crawled off of her and stood. She could feel the grip of the other two loosen and was able to turn her head and look in the direction of the newcomer. The voice came from the black cloak like rich, deep music.

"I am Ambassador of the Galactic Array, Thrapian of the 900 world alliance, and head of the universal builders' council. My name is Atromus of Perthandria." He said as he dropped his cloak to the ground. Ruth felt her soul fill with hope as she heard the title. This unexpected visitor, who had come to her twice, brought hope with him each visit. The other two thugs, sensing a fight that was about to begin, released her immediately and stood.

She scrambled to her feet and watched with rapture as Frick and and his companion charged at Atromus wildly. Atromus moved like a god. He fluidly bent his shape around the coming enemies. Although they moved with as much speed and force as they had available, he deftly maneuvered around them and did not touch them as they passed.

Atromus placed his hands together in front of himself, palm to palm. Ruth watched as the Molgothrian thugs turned around for another pass at him. She wasn't sure if she should help him, but was pretty sure she would just get in the way.

Atromus began to spread his palms apart slowly. One of the thugs swung a fist madly at Atromus as he dodged it effortlessly. The next second, he was surrounded by the three. As quickly and angrily as they tried to strike him, they could not make contact. He moved like lightning out of the way. As he did this, he continued to hold the position of his hands. His palms were now about a finger width apart, and Ruth began to notice a shimmer emanating from the gap.

A second later, As he continued to dodge the Molgathrians, the shimmering between his hands became a definite illumination. Another second and it was a bright light. The three thugs slowed their attack as the light between his palms grew. It was beyond belief but Ruth could see a fiery orb forming even from where she was.

"He's got star fire!" Frick shouted fearfully. The three stepped back now fully aware that they were in real trouble. With his hands still in the same position and his face now blazingly lit by the flaming orb in his palms, Atromus spoke to Ruth.

"Don't let them leave." His voice came in a calm tone. It took her a moment to realize he was talking to her. Now Frick was a full ten paces from Atromus. Frick was the first to try and get away with an immediate time-space jump. As the flash of light enveloped him, Ruth instantaneously sensed his wormhole and bent it back around. This time, she did not loop it back into itself because she wanted him to be aware of what Atromus was about to do.

A number of times each of the thugs tried to flash away but each time she was easily able to wrap their wormhole back to a similar location where they started. To the Molgothrians they perceived a jump but could not jump where they wanted.

Ruth was on edge as she twisted each of their jumps, but after a few successes, she was comfortable enough to realize she was now enjoying herself. She remembered that first blow that she had landed on Frick and now felt that same excitement. It was the excitement of approaching victory.

So with the thugs trapped by Ruth as a worm guard, Atromus was able to compress his star fire orb to the perfect gravitational point. She could feel the heat pouring out of it from 20 paces away.

Ruth had never seen anyone use starfire in real life but she knew what it was from the stories. Most of the great warriors used it in its various forms. She could still hear Truss explaining starfire for the first time.

"Do you know how a star works?" He had said.

"It's like fire." She replied a little unsure, which made her response sound more like a question. He laughed slightly.

"A star is a very compressed ball of fuel. Once it's ignited, it fuses light particles into heavier particles. Almost anything can be used as fuel, but the heavier the particle, the more energy it takes to ignite."

"So it's like a little star?" She had questioned, wanting to show him how smart she was, even at her young age.

"That's right, someone who can make starfire takes a small amount of their own particles and ignites them by applying a huge amount of pressure and energy. Usually, they start with hydrogen and work their way up."

She stared up at him, enthralled.

"It takes a lot of control to keep it from burning up and consuming the other matter around it. You wouldn't want to ignite a full-sized star in the middle of an inhabited world, would you?"

Knowing the answer to that one, she quickly took her cue and said, "Of course not."

"So the hard part is being able to stop it before it expands beyond control." He said.

"Is that how the rebels got star-bound?" She had said, knowing that she was on the right track.

"Hey, good job! That's right. When the great warriors would capture the bad guys, they found out that the only way to imprison them was to ignite a star with their matter and energy. It wouldn't kill them since they are immortal, but it would trap them as long as the star kept burning."

The memory dissolved as she watched Atromus now with a fully formed ball of starfire between his hands. It was hard to look at it now in its full brilliance. The Molgathrians had stopped trying to run away when they realized it was of no use. They now stood at a healthy distance and waited for their final battle. Atromus' voice came strong and forceful.

"Submit or face banishment!" He shouted with a voice that struck them more like thunder than words. The three were still for a moment. Without a word, they all simultaneously rushed in toward Atromus with a fury and rage that Ruth could not understand.

With some unseen command, the starfire that had previously been in the shape of a hand-sized orb extended out into a lengthy flaming shaft about the height of Atromus' body. He wielded the flaming blade as a master warrior, as his motions were a thing of beauty and grace. Previously, he had not allowed the thugs to make contact with him in any way. This time it was different. He spun and twisted in ways that Ruth could not even understand, and at times during the fight, all she could see was the burning brightness of the flaming saber.

The three Molgothrians tried frantically to destroy him with a myriad of desperate lunges and clumsily performed swings. With each motion, Atromus' starfire blade bit deep into the hardened flesh of its intended targets. His deliberate movements struck slash and blow time and again. As quickly as it started, it was over. The entire interplay took only seconds, but the hurricane of violence contrasted harshly with the silence that followed.

Atromus drove his blaze into the bodies of the Molgothrians numerous times before they lay on the ground in a smoking heap. Truss's words came back to her as she stared at them. These were immortal celestial souls, but from the look of the smoldering mess that lay before her, they were little more than piles of flesh. She felt a deep sadness wash over her as she looked at the three beaten thugs. How had they become so bent, she thought to herself.

In her periphery she noticed that the brilliant light of the starfire dwindled down to only a glint and then went out but she could not take her eyes off of the fallen foes. A moment later Atromus was beside her.

"I must personally ensure these three are star-bound before their bodies mend themselves." He said somberly. She thought she could hear the sadness in his voice as well.

"How did they come to this?" She said in almost a whisper. He thought for a long moment before he responded.

"Choice is a powerful thing. It makes kings of some and demons of others." They both watched the writhing heap of charred flesh for another moment before Ruth had to turn. A tear wetted the corner of her eye for only a brief second before she wiped it away. Atromus' deep, rich voice reassured her as he spoke.

"I have come because the time is near. The month is up. We must move you and your builder so that you may begin your work." He said with a shimmer of excitement in his voice. She looked at the ground as she took a deep breath and responded slowly and mournfully.

"Councilor, I have made a big mistake. I'm trying to fix it but I just haven't gotten it sorted out." She said.

"I trust that you will, Ruth." He said empathetically. "I've not been sent to assist in that matter." He placed a fatherly hand on her shoulder and waited for her to respond.

"How much time do we have?" She said with a note of fear singing through the sad melody of her question. He took a deep draft of air before he spoke.

"A final battle is coming to this world. We know that it will begin when the dark one escapes, but we don't know how or when that will be. The signs have led us to ready the war trumpets. We also know that you and your builder must be off-world by then." He said with deliberate drama.

She did not respond but instead continued to stare at the ground. After a moment of silence, he continued.

"Both of you have a great part to play in this epic, and it was not for no reason that your furlough was on this world. It is the people of this world that you build the next for." A smile crept across his face, knowing that he had just revealed a big piece of the puzzle.

She looked up at him with renewed interest. Her eyes brightened as she imagined the world that they would build. Atromus spoke again. "It will be worth it." He smiled wider as he took his hand off her shoulder.

Morning light began to stream over the horizon. She could see the glint of the sun off the broken-down gas station in the distance. She turned fully to look for James and Riley, but could see now that they were gone. She turned to Atromus and said.

"Thank you, counselor, but I have to go and get to the business at hand." He nodded as a flash of light enveloped her.

THE TREE

RILEY WAS STILL ASLEEP leaning against the tree. Apparently the excitement was more than he was used to and he was catching up on some much needed rest. His periodic snorting and sleepish moans reminded James that he was present.

Truss had decided to sit in front of the mortal man that he had revealed himself to and had since learned that his name was James. Although mostly unassuming, the fat human claimed to have a head full of Truss' most sought after treasure, his memories. Because of the symbol of good faith Truss felt deeply compelled to trust the man.

For almost two hours, James had been feeding Truss information about himself. Although the two hours had passed quickly, the amount of memory that James could access in that time frame was slowed by his human brain.

Each time Truss would ask a question about his own past, James would close his eyes and concentrate deeply.

After a few minutes he would open his eyes and deliver an answer. Truss felt sure that there must be something wrong with this human because it seemed as if this should be a simple act but it was apparently quite laborious for the mortal.

It went on in the same format of question and belated answer for long enough that James finally said, "I need a break." Up until that point, they had gained a very small amount of information for the time it had taken, but Truss had pieced together enough to understand his background, which was hugely exciting.

He was deeply enjoying the process of learning about himself, but a creeping thought was working its way across his mind. Is it supposed to be like this? He thought to himself. He could see that it would take centuries to get even an abridged version of his own history if it had to be this way.

As James took his break Truss rolled each answer he had received over in his mind. In Truss' clear perfect brain he could hear his first question as if it were being played back from a recorder.

"Why am I here?" He had said after James had briefly explained who he was. It had startled him at first when James closed his eyes. Truss wondered if he had fallen asleep or fainted. Rather than rouse him, Truss simply waited, mainly because he was unfamiliar with humans. This was, after all, the first time he had ever spoken to one. Minutes later, James' eyes shot open with excitement.

"You're on furlough, your work is very taxing and after a long string of projects you were assigned some downtime. It helps you refresh and gather some new creative ideas." James had said resolutely. Truss expected more explanation but when James fell silent he realized that he would have to ask another question.

Truss could hardly decide what question to ask. Each one crowded to the front of his mind begging an answer. He weighed each carefully. Within the walls of his mind, the last answer had set his brain ablaze. He had to know.

"What type of work did I do?" Truss said greedily. As he watched James close his eyes he remembered something he had seen while in the city. An old lady whose memory had deteriorated always was losing her possessions. She would dig around in cluttered old draws and eventually she would find what she was looking for.

As James dove deep into a library of ancient memory, Truss felt as if he could hear the clatter of stuff being pushed around in that cluttered drawer. Waiting for an answer was excruciating. I've waited a hundred years patiently, but when it takes six minutes, it is beyond what I can stand, he thought to himself. James opened his eyes and offered a welcome interruption. His face was bright with discovery.

"Wow, it's incredible! You're some type of builder. I'm not exactly sure, but I found one place in your memory where you were sort of floating over this planet and doing things." James trailed off as he realized that his words were inadequate to describe what he had just seen. He tried again. "You were floating and making things happen. Or no." He paused again. "I didn't really understand the things that you were thinking, a lot of numbers and equations were mixed in, but you were building something."

Truss fell silent, not sure what question to ask next. He didn't want to move just yet. He pored over the poorly interpreted information he had just received, trying to make sense of it. Suddenly, James, almost shouting, said.

"Oh my God, you were..." He looked at the ground as he trailed off, trying to make sense of it. Returning his gaze to Truss, he spoke in almost unbelief. "You were building that... planet. The whole time, I kept sensing this feeling of accomplishment. I didn't understand it at first, but I can see it now. You were finishing up. You are some kind of world builder."

Truss felt like wind had just hit his sails at a thousand kilometers an hour. The thrill of meaning filled his bones as he imagined it in his mind's eye. He let it soak over him as he drank in the sweet sense of purpose. His heart sped, and his breathing became excited. His longing to know his former potential grew in his soul, and he felt that he would not be able to contain it.

As an unexpected ambush, the image of the green planet came into his mind. He had longed to understand what the vision of the mountain on the green world might mean. He had tried to piece together what the dream meant. He attempted to calm himself as he asked the next question.

"I've been having this vision of a green planet with an enormous mountain that stretches beyond the atmosphere. Is there anything in my memories about that?" He said almost short of breath.

Truss nearly rolled his eyes as James closed his. This time it took much longer. The minutes ticked by as James remained locked in a mental searching game. After half an hour, Truss got up and paced back and forth. After an hour, he began to wonder if James had fallen asleep this time. After one hour and seventeen minutes, Truss returned to his seated position and impatiently tapped James on the shoulder.

Three thoughts danced through Truss's mind as he did this. This was the first time he had ever touched a human. Secondly, he noted how impatient he had become and realized that this was a first as well. Tursiarily, he reiterated to himself that this was possibly the most important bit of information he could receive.

James came out of his stupor with a start. His eyes were glazed and tired and he seemed to need a second to orient himself. Truss said nothing but simply waited until finally James put a sentence together.

"I haven't found anything. It would take me years to search thoroughly, but as I've been scanning, I haven't seen anything like what you described. Most of the planets you've worked on were rocky and small. Some of them were built to spawn basic plant life, but I haven't seen any with a mountain like that." James said tiredly. His eyes now seemed to droop a little.

Truss had a difficult time sympathising with tiredness, so he hungrily asked another question. "Why don't I re-member anything from before I arrived on this planet." James' looked up with his weary eyes.

"I'm sorry, what?" He paused before he added, "This is really tiring." Truss repeated his question. James did not close his eyes this time but said. "Ruth took your memories from you and gave them to me."

How was this possible? Rage like he had never felt before flowed into his veins. His heart doubled in speed as he imagined what he would do to her.

"I need a break," James said with that familiar note of human weariness in his voice. Almost before he finished, his eyes were closed, and he was asleep. His snoring was more constant than Riley's.

Truss felt the red-hot blanket of anger wrapping around his entire body. It started in his stomach and spread to his hands. He could feel the heat rising from his head as the blood rushed upward.

From somewhere behind him, he sensed a time-space blast and a flash of light. In a fraction of a second, he was on his feet and scanning the horizon. Coming toward him was Ruth, the villain on whom he had just blamed a hundred years of loneliness, frustration, and meaninglessness. He would crush her, he thought. He had never fought before, but apparently it was a day for firsts.

JUMP

HE POUNDED THE GROUND with his feet as he charged forward. He never needed to run since he had been on this planet, and he noticed that it felt good. He poured his anger into each step as little puffs of dust billowed up from where his feet landed in the grass.

With his eagle-like eyes, he could see recognition in Ruth's face as he approached. She had been walking, but now she was stopped. Her face turned from recognition to fear as she studied the once familiar man charging at her.

He was blitzing forward with inhuman speed, and his hands were clenched into fists in front of him. She knew that what followed would not be pleasant. He must have learned what I've done, she thought to herself as she braced for his impact.

He was closing the gap quickly, but before he was within ten meters, he blasted into a ball of light and vanished. It all happened in a fraction of a second, but she could sense where he was going. His wormhole was short and strong. It was smooth and had a bluish hue in her mind's eye. She always loved the look of his wormholes. She decided not to interfere with his jump. She knew that she could twist it around easily on him, but had decided that whatever he was about to do, she deserved.

Normally, Truss would allow his wormhole to absorb his forward inertia when he jumped, but not this time. He allowed all his momentum to be transferred down the length of this jump so that when he came out of it on the other side, he would still be moving in the same direction with all his speed.

A blast of light erupted from behind Ruth as Truss burst out of his jump. In a nanosecond, he wrapped his powerful hands around Ruth's throat from behind and allowed his momentum to carry him onward as he jerked on her esophagus. She lumbered backwards as his iron grip wrapped impossibly hard around her throat. In a split second, she was lying on her back in the grass.

He maneuvered around, and instead of falling on top of him, he landed on her. In mid-air, he spun around, still gripping her throat, and put his knee across her stomach. She looked up at him, wide-eyed, waiting for whatever punishment he planned to give to her. She had feared this moment for years now and was almost relieved that it had arrived. She had imagined a hundred times what he would do to her when he found out what she had done. She felt at peace with whatever it would be.

Truss prepared to smash her as hard as he could with his clenched fist. He took note as he reared back that she was not fighting him at all. With his fist high in the air, ready to find its target, he looked into her eyes. Although his intellect was screaming enemy, his soul was whispering friend. He saw the century that he had just spent alone. With frightening force, he drove his fist downward into the grass next to her head.

She could feel him relax his grip on her throat ever so slightly as he pulled his fist back. His knee still drove painfully into her abdomen, but he removed his hand and sat upright. She dared not move but remained lifeless and still. She stared up at him with hungry eyes, waiting.

"What have you done to me?" He said in a whisper. As he finished his sentence, he deflated and slid off her stomach. He sat on the ground facing away from her. Still, she did not rise but stayed lying. "A century of wandering and I find out that it's you that stranded me here without so much as a memory of my own." He said only slightly louder than a whisper.

She did not respond but continued looking upward at the blue expanse that stretched on forever in every direction. His words bounced around in her head like little daggers. He was right, it was her fault and she deserved to be punished. As she swallowed a huge portion of self loathing he went on.

"You were the first to appear to me, ironic that you were my greatest enemy." He said scornfully while still looking in the other direction. With that, she sat up. Realizing that there had been a miscommunication, she took a deep breath.

"I'm not your enemy Truss. I just made a mistake." She said. Her words were floating in sorrow and she hoped he could sense her remorse.

"So did I," Truss said with a biting wit. "My mistake was putting any hope in you." His words cut her like starfire. She instinctively clutched at her chest where Frick had scarred her deeply. She had mended her clothes crudely with knots, but the scar beneath still stung. Now she wore two scars, one visible and one not.

"I've been trying to find a solution." She said quickly, hoping to hide the pain his words caused her. He spat his words back at her like they were foul-tasting.

"I have a solution! Restore my memories to me." He said with a deeper tone of disdain than he had previously reached.

"It's not that easy. Your memories are stored in a human brain. Their brains are not like ours. They are soft and fragile. I can't do it without killing him." She said. Now tears formed in her eyes. "I've wanted nothing more than to restore you since I made that terrible mistake, but it's beyond me. We have no right to do that to James." Her words now broke off as she began to cry. Her tears ran hot down her cheek.

Truss stood abruptly and began to walk back toward the tree where James and Riley slept. She called after him.

"Where are you going?"

"I have a friend who told me that they could do what you could not. I plan to accept the offer." He said. His words jabbed her harshly.

"Who?" she replied.

"The Archetype."

"NO!" she screamed with surprising volume. Although angry, it was enough to stop Truss. He turned and looked at her with bitterness still burning his eyes. "Truss. Please. You can't. He is bent. He stands for everything that we stand against," she pleaded.

She ran to him and kneeled down, grabbing his hands. Looking up with needy eyes, she begged him as he stared in the distance. "They still tell stories about his rebellion in every world. He doomed millions in his campaign against the alliance and the King. War is coming to this world, and he will be finally captured and beaten." She said as she gripped his hand tighter.

She could tell she was getting through to him. He looked down at her, considering her words. She continued, "You can't see him, I won't let you." She immediately knew she had made a mistake. His expressions hardened, and he jerked his hand away from her.

"You won't let me?" He bellowed. "What will you do this time? You already have my memory, will you take my sight too? Or how about my limbs?" The sarcasm splashed all over her, and she knew she was beaten. "That's what I'd expect an enemy to say."

He turned from her and began walking resolutely. She sank back to the dirt, sitting cross-legged on her feet as she watched him walk toward the tree. For a split second, she thought that he might reconsider.

He turned back toward her and said, "By the way, the Archetype is a woman." After throwing his barbed words, he turned and continued toward the tree.

She meant the words she had said. She would stop him. She was a worm guard, wasn't she? She could not allow him to willingly step into such a trap. She stood and prepared herself. She knew he would not like it, but she had no other choice.

She watched as Truss waked James. In the distance she could tell that Riley was now awake too. She could hear his loud blurting voice.

"Who is this old fart?" Truss introduced himself to Riley and explained to James that it was time to go. Ruth focused intently on Truss. She knew that she would have one chance to block his jump, and she didn't want to miss it.

There it was, a flash of light that blasted out from where he was standing. She focused her mind to a sharpened point. She could see his wormhole, blue and smooth. This one was much more powerful than the last. It was long, longer than any she had twisted before. She reached down the length of it with her mind. She found the end, almost on the other side of the globe.

She had to work quickly. He was stepping into the jump with James. He was halfway through before she got a grip on the other end. Once she had it, she pulled with all her mental strength and twisted it back. It fought her, and she struggled but was able to bring it into submission. She twisted the jump back to about a meter from where Truss and James had jumped. It all happened in a split second. The arrival flash was indistinguishable from the departing.

It took Truss a moment to realize what had happened. Riley was shouting. "Wow, neat trick! Probably more of that witch magic. Probably should get away from him, Plump-Rump." Truss regathered his wits and prepared for another jump.

He glanced in the direction of Ruth. She wasn't sure if he knew what she was doing, but he was aware that something had not worked correctly. Maybe she really could stop him. He took a deep breath like he always did before a jump.

As the flash of light blasted out, she noticed immediately it was different this time. He must have had a clue of what she was capable of because this time she knew that she was out of her depth. She slowed her passage of time in order to see the wormhole. She mentally despaired when she caught a better glimpse of what Truss had just done. Instead of one smooth blue wormhole arcing off into the distance, there were four wormholes, each thinner in nature but equally as blue and smooth.

Four wormholes was impressive but she had no time to stand in awe of his ingenuity. She had only a fraction of a second to stop him, and she had to focus. There was no way to tell which wormhole he had ridden. She speculated that he made an individual wormhole for James and himself. She knew that a wormhole could not be opened without some mass to attach to, so he must have sent something else through the other three jump paths, she thought.

She realized that she would have to make a guess on which wormhole to twist first. She picked the one that was closest. It shot off right over her head. This time, she was able to reach down the length of the jump more quickly because she knew where it ended. She twisted it back with ease.

The next one was simple enough, but she was running out of time. She sensed that the bodies were almost three-quarters through the jump. With a mighty burst, she attempted to grab the ends of the remaining two jump paths simultaneously. Her first grab was a failure. She thought she had lost them, but when they were almost through the jump, she tried one last-ditch effort.

In her frantic despair, she reached out and was able to grip both wormhole ends and twist them back. Once she had a grip, it was not hard to return them to the starting point. Again, the second flash seemed to be connected with the first, and the nanosecond was over. As the flash of light subsided, she could see what he had sent through the jump paths.

He had made an individual wormhole for James and a separate one for himself. The difference this time was that he sent Riley through the third wormhole. It took her a second to realize what he had sent through the fourth. The tree that they had been standing under was no longer where it had been planted. The fourth flash of light revealed that he had sent the tree through a time-space jump. That had to be a first.

"What the Hell was that?" Riley bellowed loudly as the tree plopped to the ground with a thud. It narrowly missed hitting him on the way down.

"What is going on?" James said somewhat more calmly than Riley.

Ruth watched the scene unfold in front of her, but her attention was trained on Truss. He said nothing but instead studied Ruth with a practiced intensity. His anger seemed to have subsided and was replaced by the intrigue of a challenge. She could see it in his eyes, just like she had watched a thousand times before. He viewed this as a problem to solve. It was a puzzle to decode. She was confident that he would solve it. She was not a well-trained worm guard, and until the night before, she had not used those skills in a very long time.

There was a definite limit to what she could do. She had just rerouted four time-space jump paths, but she knew that was her upper limit. Truss was powerful, and she doubted that she could truly keep him here against his will for much longer.

This time around, Truss took his time. He drew in a deep breath and closed his eyes. A flash of light encircled him, James, Riley, and the tree. She slowed time to see the paths and almost lost her hold on it as she beheld. Spiraling out from Truss in every direction was a spider web of thin blue chords. Each was smooth, but they were different than the last. They were not straight like every other jump path she had ever seen. Each curled and spun in a million different directions. Blue paths seemed to split off from one another at every angle possible.

How did he do that, she thought as she tried to imagine how to stop him. The spider web of blue stretched out over her head and snaked out in inky blue patterns as far as she could see. She took a closer look at the paths that were nearest her. It was true, he had seen this as a puzzle to solve, and he had solved it.

Each wormhole was not a single path but what looked like thousands of strands. Each strand only lead a few centimeters before it terminated. However, at the end of each strand another jump path began. It was defeat, she knew she could never disentangle all of the strands that he had made.

He could hide his path easily in a spider web like this. It was the most beautiful defeat she had ever seen. She watched as a million flashes of light danced around her.

The strands that seemed to be simultaneous were actually happening one at a time. He was so much faster than her that he was able to do this easily. She had never seen him do it before, and it was breathtaking.

She watched as the million flashes extinguished and the blue spider web died out slowly. She was a beginner, but wondered if any worm guard could have stopped him with a display like that.

The light died, and she was alone. He had even taken the tree. She walked over to the hole the tree had left and looked down. She knew with finality this time that she was defeated. She thought it was time to report her utter failure to Atromus and let the axe fall.

DESCENT

James and Riley were still not used to the exhilaration of wormhole jumping. As soon as they were through the leap, they both put their hands to their stomachs. The effects of being squeezed out and back into the third dimension were more than their bodies were accustomed to. They both spun around when a powerful thud and crash occurred behind them.

The tree that Truss brought through the time-space warp rested only meters away, and the dust was still in the air from the impact. James stared at it as he tried to get his bearings. The uprooted tree looked out of place here. As far as he could see, there was sand.

As he looked out past the tree and over the desert, he felt that the sand dunes looked almost like slow-moving waves in the ocean. The sun was the next thing he noticed. Was it possible that it was brighter here? It seemed to beat down so hard that his skin would crack.

"I'm hungry, Plump-Rump." Riley's voice broke his line of thought. As James looked over at Riley, he realized that the scene seemed foreign. What are we doing here? He thought as he turned his attention to Truss. "I lost my garbage bag of goodies." Riley blurted once more, but James was now studying their strange tour guide.

Truss looked more out of place than ever. When James had first seen him, his attire had gone almost unnoticed. His garb looked like it was straight out of the 1800s, and now, standing in this merciless desert, he seemed to be lost. What is he up to?

"We haven't had anything to eat or drink in a whole day, we're running out of steam," James said. Truss, who had been looking the other way almost as if he were waiting for something, now turned toward James. With gentleness in his eyes, he looked at them.

"I must apologize. I am not used to escorting humans, and I did not account for your need to gain sustenance. What portion of your vitality remains before you perish?" Truss intoned. Although the words were strange and otherworldly, James could hear compassion and warmth in his voice. It was almost as an owner might talk to a loved pet. James looked at Riley for an answer.

"You can count my spine bones through the skin of my belly." Riley bellowed as he glared at Truss harshly.

"I take this to mean you are reaching the limits of your mortality?" Truss inquired with a real note of concern. James put his hand up in a gesture that implied that the situation was not nearly that dire.

"We're OK, but we should probably have at least some water before too much longer," James explained.

"I have a friend here who should be able to help. We will see if she is able to provide accommodations for your physical needs." Truss said.

"Anyone that's gotta go this far to find a friend gots something wrong with 'em," Riley remarked sharply. James immediately blushed and gave Riley a sideways glance.

"What he means to say is, what is our purpose for being out here in the middle of the desert?" James said softly to compensate for Riley's indignation. Truss set his eyes on the horizon again as he talked.

"We are near the stronghold of Molgathra. It is the ground lair of what remains of the Molgathrian Forces. They have been bound here. I met one among them who claims she can help with our situation." Truss said smoothly, almost as if it had been rehearsed.

"The Molgathrian forces," James said, whispering to himself. It seemed familiar, although he could not remember from what. Even just the name made him uneasy. It was as if he remembered a lesson learned from an old wives' tale, but could not recall the actual story. His face must have shown his concern because Riley seemed to notice something was wrong.

"What's wrong, Plump-Rump? You heard'a the Mole-greens?" He said. James just stared into the distance, trying to bring back something about the name. Nothing was coming. Truss retrained his attention on James as he thought deeply.

"I don't know." James said in almost a whisper. "It seems familiar but..." his sentence broke off with no completion.

"Maybe you ought to dig around in his old thought stash for a bit," Riley said as he pointed toward Truss. "Probably somethin' in there about the Mogandrons."

James looked at Truss and asked, "Do you mind if I look through your memories for the name?" Truss was intrigued and was still hungry for any information available. He nodded his permission at James and before he knew it his eyes were closed and he was searching the ancient library of memories. James' face seemed to darken as his eyes remained closed.

A deep and proud voice broke the concentration. "I see you've brought your friends to see us." James came out of the trance just in time to see a dark-cloaked man walking toward them with a smile. The pale white skin of his head was covered in scars, and its shininess glinted in the blazing sun.

Truss squared off with him as he approached, not quite sure what he intended. Stathos walked toward them across the desert sand briskly. Truss preferred him to keep his distance, but when he didn't, he braced to defend James and Riley. At the last moment, Stathos threw out his arms wide and spoke in a jovial tone.

"My brother you have come home." He wrapped his arms around him in a strong embrace. With hesitation Truss reciprocated but remained tense and ready. Stathos whispered in Truss' ear as he hugged him. "This is for the benefit of your pets, we Molgathrians tend to scare the humans." Truss could feel his hot slimy breath across his neck as he whispered.

Stathos released the hug and turned toward James and Riley. Truss studied Stathos closely as he addressed the two mortals in an uncharacteristically friendly manner. Stathos reached out his hand in introduction as he addressed James.

"James, so wonderful to finally meet you." Stathos grasped James' hand firmly. James could feel the coldness in it. A patchwork of scars covered even his hand. Alarm bells were sounding in his head as if he had just taken the hand of the devil. As he shook the cold hand, Stathos said, "My many brothers' admiration for you grows daily. They have a name for you. It's James: Seer of Ancient Secrets." James watched Stathos' face with trepidation as he shook and then released his hand.

Stathos then turned to Riely. Doing the same, he said, "They have named you Riley: Speaker of Difficult Truths." Although Stathos reached out his hand, Riley did not shake. He simply kept his hands at his side and stared at him sharply. Stathos smoothly glided over the tense moment by stepping back and addressing them all.

"I usually stay sub-materialize, but for our special guests, I felt the occasion called for a proper meeting, and it's hard to meet if I'm invisible." Truss felt like he was looking at a different person than he had previously met. He watched Stathos as he addressed them and thought he seemed almost giddy. How could he have gone through such a transformation? Stathos continued.

"These are exciting times. The many millennia that we've been bound here, we have never once been as close to victory as we are now." Stathos's demeanor darkened slightly as he paused briefly and then continued. "It is, however, still a high-stakes game. Even early this morning, we had three of our brothers fall beneath the starfire sword of an intruder. They now rest star-bound on the edge of the galaxy."

Stathos then lowered his head and made what looked like a ritualistic gesture. He placed the four fingers of his left hand on his forehead with his thumb pointed outward. With his hand on his head, he said, "May the Archetype rescue them from their eternal torture." Stathos removed his hand from his head and made eye contact with James. His tone of voice became brighter.

"To enter Molgathra, one must come willingly," Stathos said as he studied James' eyes carefully. He then turned his gaze toward Riley and waited for a response.

James timidly spoke up. He directed his comments at Truss. "I don't feel good about this. If you could give me more time I could search your memories a little deeper to see if I can find anything about them." Truss was about to speak but Stathos interrupted him greedily.

"Time is something we have very little of. The Archetype requested that you be here days ago, but he has been patiently waiting for your return." Stathos said.

"Don't you mean She?" Truss asked abruptly. Stathos placated and bowed slightly as he responded.

"My apologies, I am overjoyed at your coming, and I misspoke." Stathos stepped forward a small step and continued his plea. "I really must protest about wasting more time. We must take action or we will all be overwhelmed and star-bound by nightfall. So I ask again, will you come willingly into Molgathra?"

James, like a deer in headlights, looked at Truss for guidance. Truss said nothing but simply stared back in inquisitive patience. He then looked at Riley for his assent. Riley shrugged. James considered his options for a long moment before he responded.

"Because my friend Truss believes you, we will willingly follow you into Molgathra," James said in a more formal voice than he had intended.

"I'm still hungry!" Riley croaked as they began to walk down the crest of a sand dune.

ARCHETYPE

THE ARCHETYPE PACED BACK and forth in his chamber. His body glinted in the dim candlelight of an ever-burning wick. The few scars he wore on his exterior could not mask the deep, golden bronze of his reflective skin. Shafts of milky light reflected off of his enormous frame in every direction as even the candlelight jolted away and danced on the nearby walls. He watched the light reflect around the cave chamber as he thought of his own grandeur. He had watched kings fall at his feet a thousand times.

His powerful stature filled the height of the cave room. He knew that by the end of this day, he would know his fate. His strategy would either work or it would not. He would either escape or be captured. He shuddered as he imagined what they would do to him if he were caught. He could see it in flashes of white and red. They would ignite his life force into the densest star the galaxy had ever seen.

He would then be star-bound just like all the warriors who had been foolish enough to be captured.

He saw again the thousands that had submitted to his reign. He had taken on many names in the years of his exile on this planet that now seemed to only be a symbol for his treason. In his mind, he could see the thousands of temples built in his honor under names like Amun-Ra, Baal, Zeus, and Jupiter. His only regret was that he could not show himself in his own full glory to the humans.

He had to hide behind these names; these names that belonged to others. Those others that in their self right-eousness had bound him to this world. It was true he had borrowed the names from his brothers but he had been worshipped.

As he played back the numerous scenes from countless centuries, he could see them bowing down to him, but it never seemed to be enough. He wanted more. He almost could not believe that this would be his last day of captivity here. He thought through the details of his strategy once again.

If his plan worked, however, it would be worth every hour he had spent bound to this stinking meteorite. He imagined the look on the faces of the galactic council as he laughed a deep, bellowing laugh. He imagined the pain he would cause. This would get the attention of even the King if it worked. If it worked, he thought over and over.

"The world builder has arrived," came a voice from the corridor. "He has brought the two humans as well."

The Archetype did not even look up. He took a deep breath and walked toward the corner of the room. With each step, his appearance shimmered slightly. His strong bronze skin transfigured slowly. The scars faded away and were replaced by wrinkles. His powerful stature withered down like paper in a fire, until in its place stood the bent form of an old woman. Hair, grey and shiny, grew from the scalp in jagged tufts. The specter kneeled in the corner of the candlelit chamber and waited for the world builder and his two humans.

MOLGATHRA

This time, on their way into Molgathra, things were different. There were no juggernauts to escort them in. There were no speeches about how they must not say a word. Stathos simply showed them the way, and they followed.

James and Riley expressed their intense concern when Stathos led them through the ground in an enveloping bubble of sand, but still they followed. Riley mentioned his ever-present hunger a number of times before they reached the entrance of the underground cave.

"Where are the guards?" Truss asked when he saw there were no war giants waiting in the rock corridor of the cavern.

"They are away to make war. These are exciting times, truly exciting." Stathos said as he led them through the place where there had been 16 juggernauts the last time Truss had passed that way. They took another few steps through the passageway before Stathos turned around and stood in the path. They all stopped as he spoke to them. "Truss, I believe you remember the way. I will jump ahead and notify the Archetype that you have arrived."

"Is it safe?" Truss asked with a heavy note of concern if not for himself, at least for his friends. James and Riley waited eagerly for the answer.

"You will find that the previous population of Molgathra is quite absent," Stathos said evenly. A flash of light filled the corridor, and Stathos was gone. They all stared dumbly for an instant before anyone spoke.

"The worm guards must be gone too," Truss said. When neither James nor Riley made any response, he turned around and faced them. He could see the signs of fear on their faces as they stood trembling. Truss also noticed that their eyes seemed to be wandering without any focus. "Is there something wrong with your eyes?" He said when they could not seem to find him.

"It's darker than a tar pit at midnight in here." Riley blurted. His voice seemed to bounce off the walls forever. Truss reached out and placed a hand on each of their shoulders. They jumped in startlement when he touched them, but grasped him firmly when their hands found his.

"Come, I will lead you by the hand," Truss said. They both stepped forward as he pulled them into the darkness.

They walked through the artificial night for a number of minutes before anyone spoke again. With more shakiness than he intended James said. "What are we doing?"

"The person I was telling you about lives down here, She said she could restore my memories if I brought you to her." Truss said with iron in his voice. They walked on in silence for a another few steps before James spoke again.

"I wish you could have met Ruth, she would have helped us. She said she has been looking for you for a few years." James said. His voice was innocent and naive, but his words cut like a razor-edged knife.

Truss said nothing, but his mind kicked into high gear. He felt a pang of remorse for his brashness with her. He had not even given her a chance to explain herself. A wave of regret slammed into him, but he stood his ground.

We are doing the right thing he told himself and he was utterly convinced it was true. However, he realized that he hadn't needed to treat her the way he did. He wasn't sure if she was an enemy or not but he knew he needed to find her when this ordeal was done and have a good long talk.

"How deep we gotta go 'fore we get to Hell?" Riley blurted as his words bounced off the stone walls. They emerged from the narrow passageway into the massive cave chamber where the hoard of ten thousand Molgathrians had been gathered on Truss's last trip in. The entire room was now empty. Truss paused in the path as he took in the scene. James and Riley bumped into his back but then stood still and waited for him to continue.

They have all gone to war Truss thought to himself. Who were they at war with? He imagined the ragged legion of naked creatures marching out to battle. It must have been a hair raising sight to see.

An instant later, they were on their way. The chamber seemed almost peaceful without its vile inhabitants screeching at him. Truss wondered if the golden prisoners embedded in the walls had been released. He would know soon enough. They walked on for what seemed like hours. James and Riley did not say much. They held Truss's hand tightly.

Truss's pondering was answered when they came to the prisoner's corridor. All the bronze-skinned creatures still stood with their heads, arms, and feet frozen in the rock. For once, Truss was glad that his human friends could not see this eerie scene. The bronze skin of these shining giants was smooth and seamless. The huge warrior's bodies seemed to Truss to glow faintly. He imagined how many Molgathrians it must have taken to capture these enormous bronze warriors.

His eyes rested on each of the metallic warriors as they passed them one by one. Truss imagined the billions of stars the ancient creatures must have seen on their many adventures, like before some of the warriors still struggled against the rock, obviously not resigned completely to their captivity. Truss wondered what it would take to free them.

Even after they had long passed the chamber of the prisoners of war, Truss continued to see them in his mind. He almost didn't notice when they had finally reached their destination. He instinctively paused outside the Archetypes' chamber. This time, the huge stone door was already in an open position. The light streaming out of the gap in the passage gave James and Riley something to focus their eyes on. They finally felt stable enough to let go of Truss's hand.

Truss looked at his two human companions and nodded. He then turned and walked toward the aperture.

MEMORY

Truss' eyes scanned the small candle lit chamber as he passed through the massive rock doorway. The anticipation of the moment rocketed his mind into a heightened state of awareness. He first caught a glimpse of Stathos standing cross armed beside the door. He said nothing as he watched the outsider come in slowly.

Truss turned his eyes toward the other end of the chamber and fixed them on another familiar face. The haggard woman seemed older than the last time he had seen her. It had been only days, but her leathery skin seemed to hang looser than it had. Her deep-set wrinkles surrounded her eager eyes.

Following Truss through the doorway, James and Riley almost snuck. Their eyes were hungry for light after their long walk through the black corridor. They stood against the wall sheepishly as they took in the scene. Truss glanced back at them for an instant and could see their fear as if it were written on their foreheads.

They both cowered against the rock wall and kept their eyes on the floor. Even with the limitations of their sensory organs, they could tell this place was not welcoming.

"I'm pleased that you have come, at long last." The woman's voice croaked. Her words strained at the end as she attempted to stand. Her feet dragged the floor as if her feeble legs would buckle under the weight of her thin, ancient body. Truss watched as she moved toward him.

"I am willing to do what you asked in exchange for what you offered," Truss said. As he looked into the eyes of the Archetype, he began to wish that he had stayed with Ruth longer. The old woman made him uneasy, and he knew that she was hiding something from him. She came to a stop a few steps away. He said, "What do you plan to do once you are no longer bound to this world?"

"Have I not told you this? I once danced along the atomic pathway of the stars. I bathed in the golden light of the brightest galaxies. I could traverse the deep expanses of space in a single step. Even you can imagine, with your limited mind, what it must feel like for one like me to be bound here." She reached out and placed her hand on Truss's cheek. The light touch filled him with warmth. He held his gaze on hers and found it intoxicating. "I do not see things as you do. I can see even now, my end is approaching. Please let me be free of this place before I reach it."

As if their minds would not allow them to perceive what was happening in the room with them, James and Riley continued to look at the floor. They could hear but did not understand. They could see the shadows of these strange ones dancing across the floor, but their minds would not let them accept what was before them. Only fear had them surrounded now.

"You promised to restore my memories," Truss said in a whisper. His powerful voice seemed to be broken, and in its place stood only a weak, wispy breeze. He thought he could see Stathos smile in his periphery, but he could not turn away from the Archetype.

"Would one like me not keep his promise?" She asked as she added to the depth in her eye. With her words, Stathos stepped toward the two humans who stood impossibly close to the wall. He placed a hand on each of their heads. They both jumped with fear as Stathos placed his large palm and wrapped his iron fingers around their heads. "My servant will give you what you have earned when I am safely away." She said smoothly. Truss thought he sensed a change in her voice. It no longer seemed cracked and ancient.

"I agree to these terms," Truss said with even less strength than before. He felt that with that statement, he gave up what remaining power he had. As he did, the figure in front of him began to change.

"I will leave this world as I really am." She said as she transfigured herself. The wrinkles faded from her face as a metallic golden hue began to spread across her skin. Even then, her gender no longer seemed to be accurate. The Archetype grew in stature. With her bronze hand still stretched out and laid against Truss' cheek, she now towered over Truss as if he were only a child. Truss stared up at the Archetype in utter terror. He could never have imagined such a splendid creature.

It was as if light was pouring from every centimeter of her body. At once, Truss felt he must be in the presence of a majestic being worthy of worship. In all the widest, deepest corners of his mind, he could have never conceived of such a beautiful creature.

Dark, thick hair adorned The Archetype's head. The deep-set features of her face matched her powerfully muscular figure. He realized that to think of her as a female was not accurate. She was more like the embodiment of beauty, but she was no more female than male. Truss could not help but consider her masculine as a default. Every line of the Archetype's enormous body was perfectly proportioned. He or she, Truss was not sure which to think, wore only a tunic wrapped around his body.

Now that he had shed the specter of the old woman, the Archetype stared down at Truss. His eyes seemed to burn with the heat of a hundred stars. It was as if the powerful lines of his face were not fashioned after a concept of perfection, but instead, it was this face that was the firstborn among all the beautiful beings. It was as if the Archetype was the standard by which all things beautiful were measured. Truss could not imagine a single thing in the universe that could be so magical to look upon. It was for this reason and this reason alone that he knew it must be wrong.

His mind wandered through what seemed like a deep fog. How could it be wrong? He could imagine following this creature to the end of time. He could see himself falling in line with the countless others locked in eternal battle for this one magical being. However, he knew deep in his thumping heart that this was not his god.

Truss saw a path laid out before him. He saw the everlasting expanse of space as a place of creativity and wonder. He saw himself creating worlds in the expanse of endless night. He saw himself bringing light, shape, and form to the endless reaches of worlds yet unknown. He loved what he saw. His own eternal future flashed in his mind. As he imagined this path, one phrase among all the noise whispered itself into his soul. "For the King."

He did not know what it meant, but he knew it was the path he wanted. He knew that this golden creature that now stood before him was not and would never be his king. Although his mind could not tell him of the details, his soul spoke loud enough into the darkness that was now growing in him.

"Open the portal." The Archetype said. His voice was like thunder, and it echoed off the walls of the cave in every direction. Truss tried to resist the power of the magical voice. It was as if he were utterly compelled to comply. With as much strength as he could muster, Truss spoke weakly.

"For the King, I will not." He watched as the face of bronze changed in demeanor. Truss tried to step away from him, but with speed unlike anything Truss had ever seen, the golden hand moved from his cheek to his throat. The Archetype's hand wrapped sharply around the entire span of his neck and gripped hard. A shriek came from somewhere in the room. It took Truss a second to realize it was not his own voice.

"I've seen him in your memories. His name is the Archetype of Evil." James said with intense urgency. Truss could hear the fear screaming out through his vocal cords. He tried to speak again, "He's the one that..."

Before James could say any more, Stathos flexed his hands around James and Riley's brittle skulls. Truss could hear a loud crack as Stathos' fingers dug deep into the flesh and shattered the bones of the two humans' heads. He could not bear to look as they, his two friends, now bleeding and limp, fell to the cold stone floor. With one simple squeeze, James and Riley were dead.

Truss suddenly rediscovered his power. With all his might, he shouted. "I will never carry you from this world. You will lose this war." He grabbed at the forearm of the Archetype and tried to wrestle himself from his grip. It was like struggling with an iron statue. The Archetype was unmovable.

"I only needed your body, not your consent." The Archetype said with a booming resound. He then turned his face to Stathos, who was still standing over the dead bodies of James and Riley. He said. "I trust you got the information we needed."

Stathos looked up with splattered blood on his face and smiled. With victory in his walk, Stathos stepped closer to the Archetype. As Stathos extended his gore-covered hand, the Archetype lowered his head enough for him to reach. He placed his bloody palm on the crown of the Archetype's head.

Truss' memories streamed into the Archetype's mind. He could see every second of a life that Truss had wished for a hundred years to see. Truss could feel the burning rage as it swelled inside him, but he could do nothing. Within seconds, the transmission was done, Stathos stepped back, and The Archetype straightened. He fixed his stare back on Truss as he spoke again.

"It is time." He whispered.

"Yes, master." Stathos echoed. "I will not let him follow you."

Truss could feel his mind being invaded. One by one, his memories began to be restored. He could remember his birth. His heart jumped as the sights and sounds came back to him in jagged jolts. He could see his home world with its orange, amber glow. He could hear the sound of his mother as they ate a meal together.

One by one, his memories jumped back into his mind in rapid succession. For a moment, he lost himself in the glory of it. It was as if he were living his life all over with extreme speed. He saw his first space jump, his first assignment, and the first time he met Ruth. When he saw her face, he paused. New memories were finding their place in the bedrock of his mind, but he stayed with Ruth. He turned the memory over in his mind.

They were partners. He could see it coming into place now. He had built his first world with Ruth by his side. He recalled how tiny it had been. They were so excited to have finished a world that they celebrated ridiculously by swimming in one of its liquid methane lakes. It was an ugly little world, but they were proud.

He was swallowed up so deeply by the transfer of mind that he was temporarily distracted from the situation at hand. Now that Truss had allowed him in, the Archetype was in his mind fully. Because Truss was distracted by the upload, the Archetype had free rein of his body. Using the world builder's body, the Archetype opened a channel somewhere deep into space. He turned to Stathos before he stepped through the open portal.

"I will return with our fallen brothers." He said.

Truss felt the familiar sensation of creating a wormhole. Like waking from a dream, he was disoriented. His memories were still blasting into his mind at a million kilometers an hour, but he knew something was wrong. He could feel the blue portal arching away into deep space. He tried to quiet the noise in his mind to remember what was going on. Just slightly above the noise of the newly created memories, he heard in his mind the word King.

Just as the last memory took its place, Truss broke from his stupor and jolted out of his daze. Truss, in a frantic state, froze time around him just in time to catch a glimpse of the Archetype. He could see the blue light of a time-space jump path and knew from its width that it was a long-distance jump. He could tell from the pattern of the wormhole that it carried his own signature waveform. The Archetype was using his wormhole signature to jump off world. This would allow him to get past the worm guards that surround Earth and be free in open space.

Even though Truss had frozen the time-space around him, the Archetype was still moving forward. As quickly as he could, he attempted to close the wormhole, but it was too late. The Archetype squeezed through the closing aperture in time-space and was gone.

Truss's mind reeled at what he had just done. He had allowed himself to be taken in and deceived by the Archetype of Evil. He knew that he would live with this shame for the rest of his existence. Now with his memories intact, he thought of the stories that were told on his homeworld about the Archetype. It was unthinkable that he had just allowed him to escape.

BATTLE

WITH LIGHTNING SPEED, SOMETHING hit him from behind. With a thunderous crash, he slammed into the cave wall. He could hear the cracking and the breaking of rock as his body embedded into the stone. The gush from the impact blew the candle out and destroyed the wall of the room. Rocks crackled to the floor as Truss broke free of the rock wall.

Stathos stepped back from where he smashed Truss into the wall and made for another pass. This time Truss was ready, he spun out of the way and allowed Stathos' momentum to carry him into the wall breakage where he had just been.

Truss stood his ground and allowed Stathos to return to his feet. When Stathos found the ground again, Truss spoke a simple phrase that he had been taught for wartime. He had never had to speak it himself, and it felt strange to hear the words come from his lips.

"The King rebukes you, brother." Truss did not expect the phrase to do any good. In all of the campaigns he had heard of, there was never a time when mere words had changed one of the dark ones' minds. The galactic council insisted that every creature, no matter how darkened, deserves a trial before they are either banished or star-bound. Stathos just had his trial in that one phrase, but as expected, it changed nothing.

"My king just left to free his army from the stars. I know no other king than him," Stathos said, acid spilling from his voice. The words seemed to split Truss like a saber. How could any who had seen the true King say such words? The Archetype was majestic, but it was only an ancient reflection of the King. Truss felt an inner sickness at his words. A burning rage burst from inside him.

As if they both knew what came next with perfect symmetry, they clasped their hands palm to palm as in a single clap. Each watched the other as they sacrificed some of their body to create starfire. Truss could feel the burn growing between his hands as he began to first separate and then fuse the hydrogen atoms from his body. He could sense the heat as it began to swell. Applying tremendous pressure, he felt the presence of helium fusion in the miniature star he had just created.

Truss's Starfire was ready first. With an amazing amount of control, he elongated the flaming mini-star to a point and prepared for battle. Stathos' fire was active in short, order, although, his did not take the same shape. Stathos released the orb of fusion fire into the air. It only remained connected to him through a thin stream of flame.

He began wielding it like a medieval chain mace. Stathos began to twirl the ball of fire slowly at first but within seconds he had it spinning around him like an orbiting sun moving unimaginably fast. It moved at such tremendous speed that it looked like a shield of fire.

It suddenly occurred to Truss that his opponent had fought thousands of battles and remained uncaptured. Truss, however, had never fought one. He thought that this might be an unfair fight.

Imitating the style that Stathos was using, Truss began to twirl his starfire sword around himself at high speed. He felt that the effect was probably not as impressive as what he had seen Stathos do, but it might suffice for now.

As the fight ensued, Truss quickly realized that the order of business was more about staying out of the way of his opponents' orbiting flame. The interaction quickly turned to a high speed ball of chaos. What Truss lacked in technique he made up for in speed. He learned that he was more reflexive than Stathos but although he could stay out of the way be had no way of getting close enough to strike.

Truss made a few bad swipes at him that forced him backward toward the cave wall. Stathos' starfire quickly melted the rock wall into dripping molten lava as it dug deep gashes into the stone. Stathos lunged back, leaping from the wall laterally. Truss dodged the charge but was struck sharply by a pass of his glowing orb.

The fire bit into him violently. It sent deep waves of pain and heat through his body. He could immediately smell the burn of flesh and fabric where the fire had grazed him across his chest. He suddenly felt a deep-seated fear come over him. He feared the flame. Truss's approach became more defensive. His clothes shimmered as he continued to fight.

They stayed locked in this exchange for what seemed like hours before Truss finally landed a blow. They had melted through the wall of the small cave room and moved into the main chamber. Stathos turned sideways to leap from an angled bit of rock. When he did, he left his flank exposed. Truss took opportunity and moved in.

As Stathos became airborne, intending to fly over Truss' head, Truss sank his fire deep into Stathos. He swiped the blade, and it entered his body above his hip, traveled diagonally down, and came out on the other side. It was strange.

Truss had expected to meet some resistance when it passed through his opponent's body, but there was none. It felt no different than swinging it through mid-air.

Quite unintentionally, as Stathos was still flying through the air, the top of Truss' sword grazed and cleaved off the end of Stathos' right foot. Now with his cloak completely ripped and his foot severed, Stathos slowed his orbiting mace. Truss saw another opportunity in it and charged in.

The trap was set, as Truss moved in close, as Stathos spun around and dug his blaze deep into Truss' abdomen. The pain was immense. It shot out in spires in every direction. Truss bounded backwards from the pain. He looked down for a split second. A hole about the size of his fist was burned into his midsection. It felt like the fire was still burning him up from the inside.

Not able to compose himself, he stepped backward as quickly as he could. The pain was so intense he began to lose grip on his starfire. Stathos watched as he wobbled and nearly fell.

"Not quite accustomed to the burn of starfire, are you?" Stathos said with a laugh in his voice.

Trying to courageously face his own demise, Truss made the decision to stand his ground. However, when his starfire blaze sputtered and died he changed his mind. The pain had made it impossible to keep the proper spatial pressure on the flame and it sparked and died leaving him with nothing to defend himself.

He decided the only course of action at this point was to retreat, so he turned and ran. His speed was slow and plodding. He got to the hall of captives before he again felt the burn of Stathos' flame. This time, the orb cut his foot out from under him.

He twisted as he fell. Now, on the ground in a dark cave, he could see the face of his enemy lit only by his weapon. Truss scrambled backwards on his back, trying to get away. The fresh wound burned as he scraped it across the rocks.

"My king rebukes *you*," Stathos said with an evil irony ringing out from his bitter words.

Truss, in trying to move backwards, felt something hard against his back. As he glanced back, he saw it was the bronze body of one of the prisoners of war. Knowing he had nowhere to go, he looked up at the massive captive enshrined in the rock. His head, arms, and feet were buried deep in the stone wall. If only you could help me, my brother, he thought to himself. The golden skin shone in the light of Stathos' starfire mace, but he did not budge.

With full access to his memories, Truss now knew the origin of these massive warriors that remained locked in the rock cavern. They were the star born celestial soldiers

of the King sent to protect the world from the Molgathrian hoard, and to keep the bound ones on Earth until the
day of the Great War. Truss could hear the familiar words
of the ancient stories playing in his head.

The golden gods captured, from on high and brought be-
low.

The Warriors of the king, imprisoned and tortured by
their foe.

The shining frame of these great stars will blaze no more.

Until released from their captivity on the eve of the great
war.

He had never really understood the stanza before.
Truss's quick intellect put the stories together with what
he knew of Earth. Hundreds of human stories of mythol-
ogy talked of the war of the gods. In most, brother fought
brother to bind them below.

Truss realized that the humans must have had, at some
point in their history, known of the great and mighty
things that happened in the unseen dimension. Years of
twisting the story allowed it to sink into myth and legend.
The Archetype's brothers, had bound him to the Earth,
but in the battles that ensued he had in turn bound his
own brothers here.

"Just think, in a few minutes you will be locked in rock just like these golden giants," Stathos said as he now stood over Truss with his weapon ready. Truss felt the sharp pang of being defeated. He had known himself for such a short time, and his first act as Truss was to be beaten.

With finality, Stathos raised his mace and brought it down harshly. While the ball of fire and its flaming chain were still at the apex of their swing, Truss reached out and touched Stathos on his severed foot. With split-second speed, Truss created a wormhole and pushed both himself and Stathos through. The jump was so quick that Stathos hardly even noticed it had happened. The leap through space only moved them about 1 meter upward into the air.

Now that Stathos was 1 meter up from where he had previously been his hands that directed the starfire came in contact with the wall that imprisoned the huge golden warriors. Truss had jumped him through space just far enough so that his starfire would melt the wall around the arm of the war giant.

Truss hit the ground first, dumbly, but Stathos landed on his feet. He lost control of his starfire and it was no longer in his hands. They both looked up at the rock wall above where the enormous prisoner of war stood. A molten gash was still glowing in the rock.

With a crack and a heavy heave, the bronzed prisoner's arm broke loose of the wall. With incredible power and speed, the golden shining arm shot out of the rock wall and gripped Stathos around the torso. With unimaginable power, the arm repeatedly smashed his body against the rock. The arm of the war giant used Stathos as a makeshift jackhammer to break himself free of the stone wall. Over and over, he pounded his body into the rock until it was all cracked and broken.

When the rock wall was completely shattered around where he had been, the golden war giant stepped out into the passageway and dropped Stathos' broken body to the ground. The massive creature was not completely unlike the Archetype in size and strength. Although he was impressive, he was not as intoxicating to look at. The golden warrior's words came as a relief.

"For the sake of the king." His enormous voice filled the corridor. Truss repeated the words in like manner but said nothing else. The warrior said, "My name is Zath. Thank you for freeing me, I must now free my brothers." He paused for a second to look down at the broken mess that was what was left of Stathos. "Would you like me to take care of that?" He said as he pointed to Stathos.

"Yes, I have other business here," Truss said as he looked down as well. "He must be star-bound. He did not heed the rebuke."

"I will see that it is done as you have said," Zath replied. He then turned and began to smash the wall that imprisoned his brother warriors. Truss watched for a short time before he turned and walked.

Truss could hardly assimilate what he had just seen into his mind. He never imagined in all his years that he would be part of such an epic fight. He tried to calm himself as he walked toward the chamber where he was headed.

A moment later, Truss stood over the bodies of James and Riley. Their skulls had been crushed. As Truss looked down at the bloody bodies, he realized that this was his own fault. These two men would not be dead if it were not for his own selfishness. He wept.

Huge tears of hot, salty fluid charged down his cheek. He could see it clearly in his perfect memory, as he remembered the stories of this sad but noble race. The Archetype had stolen from them their rightful place in the galaxy. He mourned not only for the passing of these two men but for the loss of ten millennia.

He saw a dark connection in the passage of his own time on Earth. He had wandered aimlessly, slave only to his instinct to observe. Like the human race, it had led him only to a place of frustration. He could see himself in the human race. He could see their striving to become what they could not achieve. In his time here, he could see that humans instinctively knew that they lacked the intended grandeur. They, however, had no ability to do anything about it on their own.

He imagined the ten thousand-strong Molgathran horde marching to war. He needed to warn Ruth.

Truss touched James and Riley gently. A flash of light enveloped the chamber, and the three vanished.

CELESTIAL

RUTH AND ATROMUS WERE waiting for Truss when he arrived. Somehow, she knew he would return to Anberlin Valley. In the grassy valley near where the tree had once stood, Ruth had been scanning the horizon for quite some time when a bright flash of light caught her eyes. She turned in the direction of the time-space blast. Truss, with burned clothes and a substantial hole burned in his stomach, stood. His wound was healing quickly, and he seemed preoccupied with something on the ground.

She did not see James and Riley standing with him and immediately assumed the worst. Something in the grass nearby had his attention. Ruth waited for him to look up. When he did, she could see across the distance that he had been crying. At that moment, she knew.

Ruth and Atromus walked to him somberly. Ruth wanted nothing more than to run and wrap her arms around him, but she knew that he needed to absorb this all in his own time. She was glad for her own sake that Atromus was able to join her for this. She didn't know what to expect, but knew that Atromus had fought in many battles. He would know what needed to be done. Now standing near Ruth, Atromus, and Truss stood quietly over the bodies of the two dead humans.

"They trusted me, and I got them killed," Truss said in a dark tone of remorse. What he had done was beginning to sink into his mind now. The tears were gone for him, but now Ruth was getting misty. She also felt solely responsible for involving James in this whole mess.

"How did this world get so bent?" She said quietly. "How can this type of thing happen to creatures with such hope and promise?" Her tears came relentlessly now.

"This is the price for the war that has been raging here," Atromus said. His deep, rich voice was calming. Almost as if he had been broken from his daze, Truss looked up at Atromus.

"It is an honor to have audience with you, Councilor, I am truly sorry it had to be under these strained circumstances." Truss said. He made eye contact with the Councilor for a short moment and then glanced at Ruth. He could see in her eyes a hundred years of regret.

Truss turned to Ruth and embraced her firmly. She cried on his shoulder. Her hug felt like home. As they hugged, she put her ear to his chest and could hear the strength in his heart. She cried with relief. Her greatest fear was that the Archetype would pollute his mind. She had feared that he would never return. She had imagined him counted among the bound ones of this prison planet. Their hug was broken by Atromus' words.

"I believe it is the custom of the terrestrials to return their bodies to the ground," Atromus said with finality. Ruth and Truss stepped back and looked down at the bodies again.

"I will prepare a grave," Truss said. As the words came from his mouth, they sounded strange on his lips. He had never had to use the word grave before. It had no meaning on his home world. It had no meaning on any world but this one.

He felt selfish for even thinking of his station at a time like this, but he was certain that his mistakes would cost him. He was sure he would never build another world. Why else would Councilor Atromus have come? Truss knew the answer. He had come to decommission him. He felt a deep pain in his spirit. He had acted rashly, and now it would cost him his creativity.

Suddenly, without a flash of light, Truss could see with his peripheral vision that a number of figures stood nearby. He quickly turned, as did Ruth and Atromus, thinking that they had been found by the enemy. Facing them, however, he could see that they were no enemy.

Their bronze luminescent skin shown in the sunlight. The chiseled features of the one standing nearest revealed him to be the star born celestial that he met in Molgathra. The former prisoners of war now had all the station and stature that one might expect of a cosmological creature of power.

Zath stood strong and noble, wearing a white cloak. The star-born celestials did not traverse the universe in the way that the planet-born celestials did, and so the black robes of space jumpers were not necessary. They moved in and out of spacetime as easily as an aquatic bird might pop in and out of the water.

Truss and Ruth felt uneasy staring into the face of such a powerful being. Behind Zath stood six other star-born Celestials. Each was as impressive as the last. In looking upon them, Truss could not imagine the battle that it must have taken to enslave these star walkers. Atromus stepped forward to address the seven war giants.

"General Zath, I am pleased to see you have been freed from captivity. Your capture, as much as any, was mourned throughout the galaxies. Your absence from the fight created many difficulties that were unexpected and undesired. No doubt the council and the Elders themselves have rejoiced mightily at your release." Atromus said in a formal tone that was to be expected when addressing one of Zath's position. The booming voice that replied seemed to come from the clouds and surrounded them in an otherworldly symphony of sound.

"It is likewise an honor to meet you, Councilor. It was this young world builder who enabled our release and allowed the vanquishment of the last that remained in Molgathra. His epic will resound through the halls of time to the glory of the King." Zath said as his words echoed across the valley.

It took Truss an instant to realize that he was being spoken of. The murder of his two human friends played in his mind as he heard Zath's praise. He could not help but speak.

"Please forgive me, General, but I don't understand. I was at fault in Molgathra. I allowed the Archetype to escape off-world, and I allowed these two men to be murdered. I should not be praised, but punished." Truss said as he drooped his head low. Zath spoke in precise words.

"Your humility comes from a misunderstanding of the powers at play. It is true that you were deceived by the Archetype. It is true that the two humans were terminated, but that is not the whole truth." Zath said completely emotionless. Truss stared up at him with hope now as he continued.

"For eons, war was inevitable on this world. We have heard the stars whispering of its coming. We received word, while the first generation of man was young, that we must imprison the Archetype of Evil on this world. Our assignment was to keep him here as long as our power allowed. When the King broke the Archetype's hold on this world millennia ago, we felt that it was an ultimate victory. The King, however, foretold that the Archetype of Evil would escape and strike down one-third of the stars. We know little of the deep mysteries and did not understand it until it happened. We could neither see how the Archetype of Evil would escape, nor could he in his state of defeat. However, intending to do evil, he is fulfilling what was foretold. He is extinguishing a host of stars to release his star-bound army.

We now see that it was you who allowed his escape, unknowingly. You are free of guilt in this. It was for the sake of the King that you were allowed to be deceived." Zath turned his deeply intense gaze to Ruth and continued.

"Child, you as well have long since felt guilty for your mistake. You, too, are guiltless in this. It was for the sake of the King that this has all come to be." Zath now sped up in his explanation and addressed them all.

"The Archetype of Evil escaped his imprisonment to fulfil what was foretold, and will return with a sizeable force. The King intends to return and meet them in open battle. You must be off this world by the time this happens." Zath paused, and Atromus took his opportunity to speak.

"Is there nothing that can be done for these two sons of the earth? It was not for any fault of their own that they were involved in this." Atromus said as he pointed down at James and Riley. Zath stepped closer as his six companions stayed where they were. The ground shook when his foot touched down.

"It is for these two men that I have come. The King himself has a purpose for them. They are to be his two witnesses. They will speak truth to the world until the time of the great battle." Zath said.

"How is this possible? They are both deceased?" Truss asked.

"Reach out your hand and touch the wound," Zath said to Truss. He kneeled down and touched the bloody spot where Stathos had dug his fingers into James' brain. Truss felt ill at the sight of the carnage.

As his fingers grazed the fracture, something began to happen. A tingle of light and spark emanated from Truss's hand. He watched as the break in the skin began to close.

The skin knitted itself back together, and the wound on James' head healed. As if on cue, James took a deep draft of air and sat bolt upright. His eyes opened. Disoriented, he found Truss's face, and a smile came across his.

"Truss?" James said with a question in his voice. He then looked around and saw Zath and the six other War Giants. His breath came sharply, and he was filled with fear. He looked back at Truss for reassurance and found it there.

"Don't be afraid, my friend," Truss said as he placed his hand on James's shoulder. James took in more of the scene and immediately found the sight of Riley lying next to him with an incredible head wound. Again, James looked to Truss for assurance and found it.

Truss simply reached down as he had already done, but this time touched Riley's wound. As expected, the skin around the fracture knitted itself back together, and Riley did the same. When he took the first breath and sat up, he did not react to the scene in the same way but instead remained quiet and waited for an explanation. Truss and Ruth helped James and Riley to their feet, and Zath addressed them directly.

"Servants of the King, James and Riley, you have been chosen to carry the message of judgment and hope to this world. The wounds in your heads were allowed because you must be without fear. This will not be the last time that the best of Molgathra will kill you. However, you now know that you will not stay dead, but the King, in his deep wisdom, has power over even that. You are being sent from this place to speak truth to all the world. The King himself will teach you what to say when the time is right." Zath said.

Even as the echo of his powerful voice died, James and Riley seemed to be changed. What was merely human now stood strong as one of the few that had risen from the darkness of death, as even the King himself had done once long ago. James turned to Ruth and Truss.

"Thank you," James said with the kind of emotion that only a human can achieve. Riley simply nodded at them with a smile. A second later, they vanished from sight.

Truss felt like a million-ton weight had just been lifted from his chest. He was not, after all, a murderer. He was not a traitor. He was free of guilt. Truss and Ruth exchanged a proud glance almost as parents of a successful offspring might. They drank in the relief and joy of the moment. They could have lived in its perfection for a thousand years. Their silent revelry was broken by Zath's powerful voice.

"World Builder, you and your companion have much work to accomplish. The people of this world will need a new home. It is time to begin." Zath said. After speaking these words, the seven radiant giants were gone. Truss stood stunned and not quite sure what to do. It was Atromus that broke the silence.

"Congratulations to both of you. You have come through this trial intact for the sake of the King." Atromus said victoriously. Again, Truss and Ruth exchanged a glance of excitement.

"How do I know what to build?" Truss said.

"You have already seen the world in your mind's eye. The green planet with the majestic mountain. It is yours and your team's to build. You observed life on Earth extensively. The team you lead will create a new home for its redeemed life, for the glory of the High King. The mountain will be the place of communion between the world reborn and the city of the Great King. This new world will be a beacon to which the rest of the universe will look for a million years." Atromus said.

It seemed that there was nothing else to say. So they did not speak. Truss and Ruth bowed slightly to Atromus as a gesture of thanks and gratitude. They were all filled with the deepest sense of excitement, joy, and peace. Although the unknown faced them, Truss, for one, was ready. Atromus left them first. The flash of his jump gleamed in their eyes.

Left alone, Truss and Ruth turned. They looked into each other's eyes and wrapped their arms around each other. He leaned in slowly and kissed her. In that kiss, he poured a century of loneliness, passion, and love. He had always loved her. As they remained locked, a flash of light enveloped them, and they were gone. Their child, a green world of splendor and breathtaking beauty, would soon be born.

AUTHOR'S NOTE

THANK YOU FOR READING World Builder. This was the first book I ever wrote. Since it was published in 2012, I've written a number of other books and learned quite a lot about the craft. Even after years of writing other novels and working on other projects, World Builder still holds a warm place in my heart. It was as much an adventure for me as it was for Truss, Ruth, James, and Riley.

As you may have gathered, this book is urban fantasy/science fiction written from a Christian worldview. So much of science fiction is created from an atheistic position, and fantasy from a pagan one. Don't misread me here. I LOVE sci-fi and fantasy of all stripes. It, however, pains me to find that most of the authors of those stories do not believe in Jesus.

I recently did a book reading and asked the audience, "What is fiction?" There were various responses, but the one that stood out to me was this. "Fiction is a story that is not true," I responded with this.

"Jesus was a fiction writer." This got strange looks and produced some confusion. I explained that Jesus taught TRUTH through FICTION. Jesus told stories. In fact, his stories are probably the best-known fiction in the world. He used these fiction stories (parables) to teach some of the most important truths.

Here's why it matters. I'm convinced that Christians need to be great storytellers. Our Lord was. We so often ruin a great story by telling it poorly. We start with the ending and spoil the journey. We miss opportunities to teach truth through fiction. Often, we don't tell stories at all, but instead give a synopsis of the gospel. We weaken the truth with our ineffectiveness when we do this.

So that is my mission. I want to teach truth through fiction. I believe that there is an amazing universe of activity happening right under our noses. I hope this book (and my other books, which I hope you'll read) has brought to life something inside of you. I want readers to be excited about the world that lies underneath the visible.

I'm convinced that the most important thing that you can do in this life is, first, believe in Jesus to receive everlasting life. Once you've done that, you have everlasting life no matter what happens. That puts you in a secure place to, second, follow him for the reward he will give, both in this life and the life to come.

Other than that, I'm going to ask for a simple favor. Please review this book on whatever platform you received it from. Reviewing God-honoring books is a great ministry that any book reader can do. Once done, you can jump into one of my other books. You see what I've been publishing since I wrote World Builder by going to:

<u>LUCASKITCHEN.COM</u>

Thanks for reading, and I look forward to seeing you in the pages of another adventure soon.

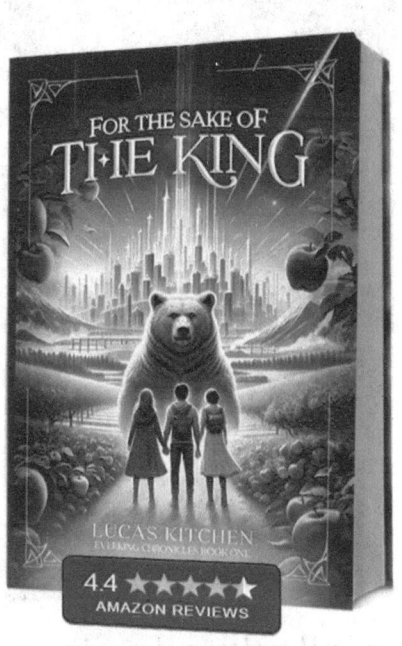

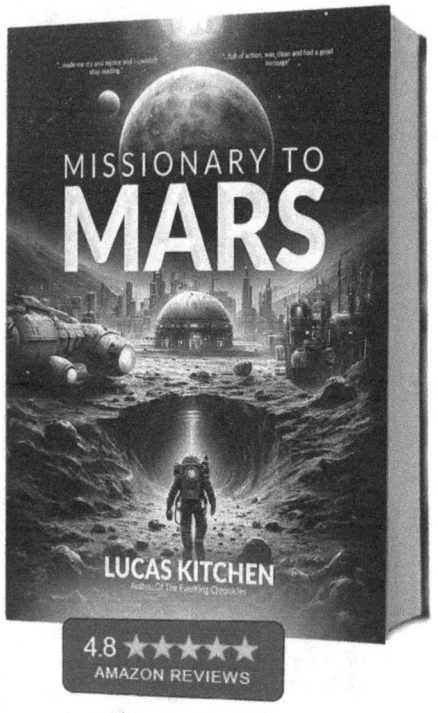

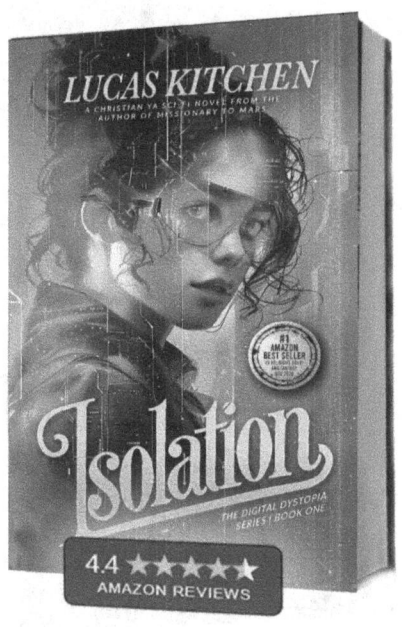

ABOUT THE AUTHOR

LUCAS KITCHEN IS AN American author of both Christian fiction and nonfiction. He has written over twenty books, and had some on Amazon's category best-seller lists. He writes blogs, releases podcasts, and publishes social media videos about Jesus, the faith, and Ai robots. His social media content occasionally goes viral. He lives in Texas with his wife, and four kids. You can see his books at Lucaskitchen.com.